DALE MAYER

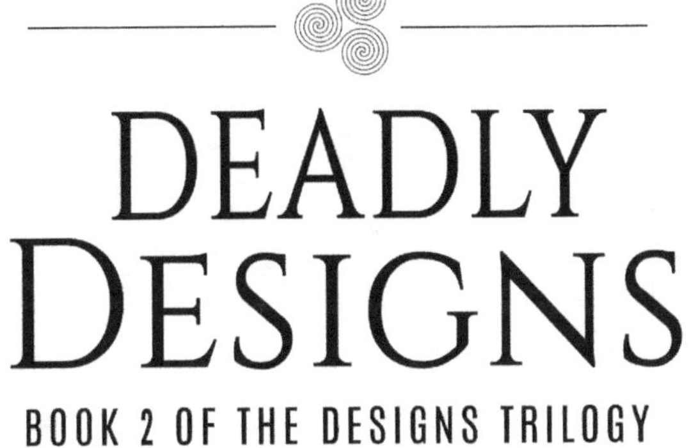

DEADLY DESIGNS

BOOK 2 OF THE DESIGNS TRILOGY

DEADLY DESIGNS
Beverly Dale Mayer
Valley Publishing Ltd.
Copyright © 2012

ISBN: 978-1-988315-98-0
Print Edition

About This Book

Drawing is her world...but when she's banished to a deadly new world and needs help, it's his world too.

Her… Storey Dalton wants to go home – but something goes terrifyingly wrong and she ends up in her worst nightmare. There's no escape…not without Eric or her stylus. Then she finds someone who needs rescuing even more than she does…

Him… Eric Jordan races to save Storey, only to realize a close family member has betrayed them both. Now the enemy is closing in on him. When he meets up with Storey, he knows her plans are a bad idea, but she won't be dissuaded…and it could be their only way of staying alive.

It… The stylus, now bonded to Storey's artistic soul, is determined to survive this new chaos – against all odds. But damaged from a prolonged separation, he can't help Story or Eric – without making things worse.

Them… Storey is determined to make things right. Eric is determined to help her. Neither counts the personal cost, until their very lives are in danger.

Sign up to be notified of all Dale's releases here!

https://geni.us/DaleNews

Dedication

This book is dedicated to my daughter Kara, who asked me to write books for her. The Design Series is the third young adult series I started for her.

Enjoy!

Acknowledgments

Deadly Designs wouldn't have been possible without the support of my friends and family. Many hands helped with proofreading, editing, and beta reading to make this book come together. Special thanks to my editor.

Prologue

In Dangerous Designs we left off with this chapter...

ALL THE WAY back to Paxton's lab and the resounding victorious welcome waiting for them, Storey had trouble dealing with the fact that it was all over. That this nightmare she'd been living for days had finally finished. So much excitement. So much panic. So many emotions had rushed through her constantly. And then everything stopped. The chaos was over. Resolved. The change so sudden...she found it hard to believe.

It didn't feel right after days of living on a roller coaster. Days of fearing for her life and Eric's, the ranger from a different dimension. Now he was safe. She was safe. Everyone in his dimension was safe.

The stylus, the odd pencil-computer thingy with souls bound inside that she'd found, had opened a portal between the Louers' old and new worlds. Only time would tell if they'd make good use of it. Her stylus assured her the Louers were exploring their new world already.

Paxton, Eric's mentor and senior council member to the Torans, had monitors that tracked any activity through the areas where the dimensional tears had been repaired until they could all be reinforced. The process would take a bit longer, but like he'd said to her, they were on it.

They were on it.

As in she wasn't needed any longer.

They'd even managed a decent conversation over the future of her stylus. Now that she knew more, she understood his reluctance to let her keep it. Then he also understood her unwillingness to die in order to give it back. A truce had been made letting her keep it until they could figure out how to separate it from her safely. She kept the fake one tucked away. Just in case Paxton decided not to be as reasonable as he currently appeared.

Instead of feeling euphoric, she felt odd, uncertain. Almost as if she expected, no wanted, more chaos. And that couldn't be right. She wasn't a masochist. Why the hell would she want more war?

Because there'd been a certain attraction to being someone respected, looked up to. Someone who'd had answers. Someone who'd learned to do something others hadn't. Her pride and self-confidence had definitely had a good time here.

And it was coming to an end.

God, she was becoming downright depressed.

Off on one side, she watched the party going on around her. It was a standing-room-only crowd. Where had all the people come from? There were some seriously beautiful women here tonight which just added to her depression. She was still wearing her old jeans and sneakers.

Even the usually formal and uptight Paxton had let loose. He'd danced and hugged his way through the crowd. With so many well-wishers, she'd hardly had a moment to herself, hence her attempt at a time-out.

Eric found her a few minutes later. He slung an arm around her and held her close. "Hey, what's wrong?"

She relaxed against his shoulder, thankful he'd joined her. She needed this – him. "Nothing." With a light laugh, she added, "I was just ready for a couple of minutes of peace."

"That makes sense." He snagged a stool and sat on it without disturbing her position. "Are you ready to go home?"

"In a way. Then again, I finally feel connected to everyone here. We've been through so much, it's hard to leave."

"It's not forever. I'll be able to come over and visit, and you'll be able to come back."

"Will you though?" If she were honest, the fear of never seeing him again was behind the sense of letdown she'd been feeling all night. With his world safe again, it was over. There was no reason for Eric and her to meet anymore, except wanting to be together. They had a relationship – she just couldn't decide what it was. But she wanted to see where it could go. And how could she do that if they lived in opposite worlds?

If long distance relationships were hard to keep, then cross–dimensional relationships would have to be impossible.

And given his father's disposition, she didn't think she'd be welcome over here anytime soon. Everyone else had been friendly though. Several people had stopped to thank her. Some had stopped to ask her questions about her world and how long she was staying.

She needed to go home. Who knew what she still might have to fix back home yet? She'd left things in a bit of mess. And undone. Like the note on the inscription of the stylus she'd hidden on her computer. Not that it mattered any more as she could just ask the stylus about the lettering. Later, when she got home and had time to delve into all the unanswered questions.

"You look like you've lost your best friend." He bent closer to peer into her eyes. "Are you okay?"

"Yes." She gave him a reassuring smile, at least she thought it was. "I'm just sad."

"That's understandable. You've made some friends here. We appreciate all you've done. We might even be able to have you come over as a consultant on some projects."

"Really?" She brightened. "I figured I'd never be welcomed back – considering I had a death sentence on my head at one time."

"A fond memory of your visit." He snickered. "Even if they aren't interested in having you consult, I'll come visit you. I promise. There's no way I'm giving up our friendship."

She closed her eyes briefly. Then said with a lilt in her voice, "Boy, am I glad to hear that. I guess I was feeling a little blue, thinking I'd never see you again."

"Not going to happen." He stood up. "But I understand you need to go home. Did Paxton speak to you yet?"

"He apologized and thanked me." She smirked. "I think he's still a little miffed at me over the stylus stuff."

Eric laughed. "I wouldn't be surprised. He's been bonded with his for over a century. It can't be easy to be shown up by a young girl. Especially one not even from his world."

"I can understand that."

Eric pulled her upright and into his arms. He stared at her quietly for a long moment. His voice rumbled from his chest. "Thank you for coming back and helping us. I'm not sure we'd have survived without you."

"You would have, just in a different way." Storey nestled closer. "I couldn't see your world suffering when I'd figured out a way to help."

"And help you did. The Louers are gone forever and all because of you."

She lifted her head to caution him. "We don't know they're gone for good. It's too early to say. Paxton still has some work to do there. He has to make sure the portals are permanently sealed. We also don't know which dimension the Louers ended up in – for sure. We *think* we do, but…"

"Paxton will sort it out. He's nothing if not dedicated." As if to calm her worries, Eric bent and kissed her gently, then with growing enthusiasm.

"Arrumph."

They broke apart to find Paxton standing in the doorway. "I think it's time. Everyone wants to say good-bye to Storey and watch her leave."

"Oh." She brushed her shirt down and walked over to where her backpack sat on the floor waiting for her. "I hadn't realized."

They walked back into Paxton's lab to find a line had formed. Most of the Torans hugged her or shook her hand. By the time she'd reached the end of the line, she could barely hold back the tears.

Paxton gave her a codex. "So you don't have to travel by drawing portals everywhere. We all saw the result of that effort!" There was mixed laughter from the crowd, but it was the warm look on Paxton's face that made her respond with a big grin.

When the laughter died down, Paxton added, "This is a guest codex. It's pre-coded for your home, my dear. Thank you for all you've done."

Tears collected in the corner of her eyes. Storey smiled mistily. She really was going to miss him. "You're welcome."

Impulsively, she gave him a quick hug.

Eric walked her over to the portal that his people used for travel and dropped a kiss on her cheek. "I'll pop over tomorrow to see how you're adjusting to being home again. Your mom has to be wondering where you've been all this time."

"True enough." Thinking about her mother brought her father to mind. Oh boy. What waited at home for her? Not daring to speak in case she broke into tears, she managed a brave smile. He reached over and hit the button on her wrist unit. The familiar musical notes sounded.

Storey straightened her back, determined to go out gracefully. Forced to sniffle back tears, she gave the crowd a quick wave good-bye. It had been a hell of a weekend. She'd miss these people. Definitely Eric and maybe even Paxton. With a final look around the room, she recognized Eric's father, the hated Councilman, standing in the far back corner, a malicious grin on his face. What was he up to? He looked way too happy for her comfort.

The black mist swirled up around her legs.

The Councilman gave her a wiggling fat sausage finger wave good-bye and opened his other hand so she could see what he held. Nestled deep in the rolls was a long thin object.

Her stylus.

The black swirling mist rose to her chest.

She gasped in shock.

It was too late to stop the portal.

His grin fattened.

The room disappeared into darkness. Panic threatened. Oh God. Was she going to die now? Could the esteemed Councilman have actually won? She closed her eyes, hating him and what he'd done. How could she contact Eric to let him know? Without her stylus she had no way to communicate with anyone here.

Just then the mists thinned and cleared.

She turned around. An oily darkness greeted her. The rank smell of death rose, overwhelming her senses. She wrinkled up her nose and coughed, then coughed again. "Oh God. I know that smell!"

Hearing something behind her, she spun around. A long meaty arm stretched through the darkness. White bony fingers reached for her.

CHAPTER 1

THE STENCH WOKE her. It spread deep into the recesses of her comatose brain like a shockwave. Storey Dalton slammed back to consciousness – and retched violently. Again and again. Finally, she groaned and collapsed to one side.

Coughing spasms came next. By the time that slowed, her thin frame stopped shaking and her stomach calmed down, Storey could lie in relative peace. Except for the smell. The sour reek of vomit now mixed with a horrible odor, almost like sulphur or rotten eggs. For a moment she just rested. Then her eyes shot open. She stared around in shock.

What the hell had just happened? Deep, depressing darkness surrounded her. She could see no lights, windows or moon around her, only complete, unforgiving blackness. She rolled to her right side and shifted to a sitting position. In a denseness where all other senses were deprived, the stench was almost enough to send her reeling to the ground again.

And ground it was. Dirt. Damp, black, hard dirt. If there were a hell, she imagined she'd found it.

Why?

How had she ended up in such a place? Events were as murky as the atmosphere around her. Eric. She'd been with Eric after helping to save his people, his entire dimension in fact, from the Louers. There'd been a party where everyone had joyously gathered around to thank her and send her off properly.

She'd been going home.

Storey struggled to her feet. Home. To her mother. And apparently after messing with the essential fabric of her own dimension, her father maybe as well. And that was so wrong. He'd been absent from her life for over a decade until she'd screwed with things. She'd tried to fix her mistakes, but hadn't had a chance to find out if her changes had been successful or not. Did her parents still believe that she attended a Roman Catholic school and did her homework on time? A snort escaped. As if. Given a chance, she'd spend all her time drawing.

She stilled. Drawing. The stylus. Eric's father, the Councilman, had stolen it. It had been in his fat hand as she'd disappeared in the portal. The mist had swirled up around her too quickly for her to yell for help. Could he have also changed her destination? Or was she being unfair? The unstable gates might have screwed up the destination. Paxton was making repairs but that didn't mean everything was working perfectly yet.

Then again, remembering the look on the Councilman's face she had to think he'd had something to do with her current disaster.

Shudders slipped down her back at the memory of long, bony hands reaching into the mist to pull her from the portal. Thank heavens she'd passed out. That's one memory she won't have to relive.

God only knew where the creatures were now.

And how was she going to get out of here without her stylus?

Hope surged inside as she remembered the fake stylus she'd created while still in her dimension. She'd made the decoy to fool those who might try to take the real stylus from her.

So had the nasty Councilman stolen *her* stylus – or the fake one?

For a furious minute she searched all her pockets. Empty. *Crap.* She whispered, "Are you here, Stylus?" She waited, hoping for that telltale tingling sensation. That sense of connectedness to the souls inside the stylus. Even though that connection hadn't been there that long, it had deepened, becoming a part of her.

According to Paxton, when a stylus became separated from its owner for a long time period, normally the owner died. Something to do with the soulbound relationship between the two.

Where was her backpack? It held her completed portals, jacket and sketchbook. Taking a few tentative steps, she tried to search around her. What's the chance her bag had been left with her?

Just then her foot banged into something hard, sending her downward where she cracked a knee against a rock. At least she assumed it was a rock. "Damn it." She jumped up and danced around in one place, afraid she'd hit something else.

"Would someone please turn on the damn lights in this Godforsaken place?"

Instantly lights blazed, blinding her. Instinctively she slammed her hands over her eyes as they burned with the severe change. "Shit," she whispered as she squinted between her fingers. The room glowed from a strange incredibly bright light source at the far side. Her eyes didn't know what to do with it. Keeping her eyes shaded, she turned slowly to look around. There was no sign of her backpack or her stylus.

The room appeared to be a huge underground bunker. Or a cave, maybe? Yet she couldn't see an entrance or an exit. And it was empty – except for her.

The reality of her situation set in.

She was a prisoner. But she had no idea where, or who held her here.

Or why.

ERIC WATCHED THE dark mist thicken, dread overtaking his senses. What could have caused that look of absolute horror on Storey's face? He stared hard at his father's rotund and positively gleeful face. Until he caught Eric staring at him. Then his fat grin slid off, his nose strutted up into the air and a look of superior disdain came over his cold features. Yeah, that's the normal expression Eric remembered.

The false face. It had taken Storey to show him the real man inside. It hadn't been easy to see. And even harder to accept. Now he just felt stupid. He'd spent his life respecting a man who deserved none of it. And adding to Eric's confusion was the realization he really didn't know this man.

His father was a stranger. Eric hadn't seen much parental love in his life. In reality, he'd had little contact with him. Since he learned to walk, he'd had respect and obedience drummed into him for a man he was only just realizing didn't deserve it.

How had the Council allowed this man to rule? What could his father have done to deserve their respect? And couldn't they see the man his father had become? Or had the changes happened so slowly that they hadn't been evident — until some major disaster when he'd shown his true self. Then again, he'd been the ruler for so long because there wasn't much to rule here. His decisions were mostly over little issues.

Still, Eric wondered about the man inside. Was he driven by power? Needing blind obedience from all like a dictator? Something Eric hadn't considered his society could have.

Storey's arrival had certainly thrown his father off balance. And had showed Eric a side of his father he'd never seen before.

Paxton on the other hand…. He glanced over at his mentor. Tufts of his white hair stood straight up, only this time from running his hands through it in excitement. Paxton was still on a high from the success of the day. His cheeks were flushed, and he appeared to be…dancing?

Eric continued to scan the partygoers. His people certainly were enjoying themselves. This mini war had restored pride they hadn't known was missing from their lives. They'd slipped into a passive type of existence. This had woken them up, stirred them to action. They wouldn't be quite so complacent about their lifestyle any longer. At least not for a while. And like them, Eric wanted to enjoy himself tonight. Celebrate today's success.

But…

Eric shook his head and spun around again to look at the spot where Storey had disappeared. He couldn't get the look on her face out of his mind. What could have caused it?

Paxton walked toward him, a lilt to his step, a bright look on his face. Eric had to grin. Paxton looked like he'd dropped twenty years off his shoulders.

"Eric! Still worrying about Storey? She'll be fine."

Eric shook his head. "It doesn't feel like she's fine."

Paxton narrowed his gaze. "Do you want to go after her? Make sure she arrived safely?"

Eric contemplated his sense of something being wrong. Did he want to go after her? Heck yes. "I wouldn't have to be gone long." He studied his feet. Was there really something wrong? Or was he just missing her? Either way, he needed to know for sure. "I don't want to make a big thing out of this if everything is fine."

"We could just ask her if she's home safe and sound." Paxton held up his stylus, a wide smirk on his ancient face.

Perfect. Eric grinned widely, relief spreading throughout his body. "Perfect. Thanks."

Paxton grabbed up a nearby pad of paper, his movements easy and carefree, as if knowing this was for naught but happy to play along. He quickly wrote out a note to Storey. Eric read the simple message. "Hello Storey, please confirm that you made it home safely."

Lifting his head, Paxton beamed. "Amazing communication ability. I just love this. There's so much we can learn from these styluses."

He sounded positively chatty. Eric struggled to reconcile this Paxton with the grim, stern version from before the war. Talk about polar opposites.

"You know, my stylus knows all about the archives. Storey says they can access all the information from centuries ago. Do you understand how much we can learn from them?"

Eric raised an eyebrow as he finally noted the rosy cheeks and the overly bright shine to Paxton's eyes. Had his old mentor and friend indulged in a little too much to drink?

Surely not? Eric couldn't remember seeing the man ever take a drink of wine.

But there was no doubt that he was under the influence of something. Maybe it was the power of success?

The stylus sat quietly as both men waited for an answer from Storey.

Eric's gaze narrowed as the moment stretched out longer and longer. "Could something be wrong?"

"Well, anything is possible, but it's unlikely. She's done this trip dozens of times."

"Ask your stylus if Storey's stylus is in her dimension."

"Why? We know it is." Some of the brightness dimmed in the older man's eyes. "You really think something is wrong?"

"If it isn't, then why hasn't she answered by now?"

"Maybe she's sleeping."

Eric blinked. Good answer. Why hadn't he thought of that? It was late. Storey had been on an incredible adrenaline rush, helping him and his men to save his world. Going home would have brought on a major crash and burn cycle. She might simply be asleep.

No! His mind screamed at him. Storey would have contacted him to let him know she'd arrived safely. She knew he'd be worried about her. There's no way she wouldn't do that.

"Please, just ask."

Shaking his head, tufts of white hair flipping out in all directions, Paxton picked up the stylus and wrote the question.

The answer was immediate. "No."

Both men shouted, "No?"

"Why not?" Paxton glared at the single word he'd written down. "She has to be."

Eric knew his father had been up to something. But what? "Where is her stylus? Maybe it's still here."

"Well, it shouldn't be. Not unless she's here, too." The answer came back immediately. Paxton read out the answer. "No. Storey and her stylus are not in this dimension."

The two men stared at each other in shock.

"We've been having problems with the gate so maybe something malfunctioned," Paxton mumbled.

"Ask where she is, please." Eric tried to contain his impatience. Though Storey had been willing and eager to find out information through her new pen as she thought of it, Paxton clung to the old ways and asking a simple instrument for help wasn't instinctive – or natural. The styluses could communicate with each other, but Eric thought Storey's was stronger and more capable. Or maybe Storey was stronger and more capable than Paxton.

He'd verbalized the questions before but now seemed to be only able to write down the questions. Either way, Paxton was working too slowly for Eric right now.

Paxton slowly wrote the question on the paper as if not wanting to hear the answer. The stylus never moved.

"See, there's no answer." Paxton sighed. "It must be a broken gate. Maybe it can't get a reading."

"What are you doing over there?"

Eric stiffened, a subconscious effect of his father's approach. He didn't dare look his sire in the eye, afraid that his suspicions would get the better of him. Surely his father wouldn't have willfully done anything to hurt Storey.

Yes, he would have.

This was the man who had once ordered her imprisonment and death. Eric's instincts screamed at him. Stay silent.

Things were bad but they could get so much worse.

Paxton opened his mouth to answer and caught Eric's glare. Slowly, as if not understanding, Paxton dropped his gaze to study the paper in front of him.

"We were talking strategy," Eric answered calmly enough.

His father tilted his head upward. "Why bother? The problem's been solved. It's not going to happen again, so sure, hash over your success, then let it go. I won't have anyone wasting their time on such things now that the war is over."

"And if the war isn't over?"

"Don't say that," the Councilman snapped at his only son. "It's over. That subject doesn't come up again, do you hear me?"

Eric struggled to keep back the words ready to blast out of his mouth. Setting his father off wouldn't do anyone any good at this point. With a clipped nod, and a last warning look at Paxton, he walked away from the men, determined to catch Paxton alone later. He needed to focus on Storey, now.

Keeping an eye on the happy partygoers still around, he checked his codex. How long had she been gone? One hour, not more. Too bad he didn't have a stylus of his own. It would be a great way to talk with her. How else were they going to communicate when they each lived in a different dimension? He had methods that worked in his dimension. Her cell phone worked in hers. But only the stylus was capable of crossing both dimensions. Checking behind him, he heard raised voices coming from his father and Paxton. *Uh oh, someone isn't happy.*

Well, neither was he. He strode back across the room to the two fighting men. His father saw him coming and rounded on him first. "I do not want to hear any more about that girl from you. She is gone and she is not allowed back in our world. Do you understand?"

Fury built inside Eric to the point that he could actually see black spots as he tried to find some measure of control. Releasing his rage at the Councilman, father or not, was liable to be a final step he wasn't sure he was prepared to take.

"No. That is not acceptable."

Eric blinked. What? Had Paxton really stood up for Storey? At one point, he'd been firm that she should return to her world and stay there. For good.

Paxton pulled up to his full height. In an authoritative voice, he stated, "Storey has been a valuable contributor to our world this past week. We have much we can learn from her."

"She caused the dratted problems in the first place. I do not want her back. Do you hear me?"

"I think everyone here heard you." Eric couldn't hold back his own anger, noting that half the partygoers were leaving and the other half were starting to collect around the arguing men.

The Councilman rounded on him, fire leaping from his eyes. "You. I've heard all I'm going to from you. I'm not sure why you think it's suddenly acceptable to argue with me, but there is no way I can consider your actions in any good light. That this young woman should have had such a disagreeable affect on you is unacceptable. You need to learn your place."

With narrowed eyes, he drew himself up to his full height. That it was many inches shorter than Eric's only made his action more laughable. No one within hearing distance could doubt that the Councilman was ready to hand out another final edict.

He opened his mouth.

"No." Paxton stood firm. "You will not punish him." Glaring at the rotund Councilman, Paxton shook his head. "You cannot. Eric is a hero to our people, as is Storey. They have become icons of hope, faith and courage. They deserve your recognition, your respect and even medals of valor for their actions."

As Paxton's words faded away, the gathering crowd picked up the energy and started to cheer, calling out Eric's name.

Eric. Eric. Eric.

Eric had to grin at the consternation on his father's face. The Councilman hadn't expected resistance. Especially from old Senator Paxton, a title the scientist never used, but still possessed; or from his own people. A red flush whispered across his father's face, his beady eyes going hard and bright with fury before sliding into cold determination. As Eric watched and waited, wondering what his father would do next, it was as if a switch had been thrown and his father settled back down.

Eric's suspicions rose again.

His father turned to face him, straightening to his full height. "So be it. We'll come up with some way to reward you for your actions, Eric."

Eric frowned. The words sounded right. The tone of voice definitely didn't. His father was up to something.

"And for Storey?" he asked, cautiously hoping his father would let something more slip.

"Oh, yes. Storey is getting everything that's coming to her."

Just then several things happened.

Paxton's stylus started moving in the air. Paxton raced to snatch up a useable piece of paper to write on.

His father grinned a sly, slow movement that sent shivers down Eric's spine. Then he turned and strode out of the room.

CHAPTER 2

S TOREY SAT WITH her back against the dirt wall. Stumped. How could she get out of this mess? Her backpack was missing and her pockets were empty.

Panic sat on the edge of her consciousness, waiting to take over. She'd come to rely on the stylus and sketchbook so much that she found herself at a loss. Her simple codex, not like the high-tech one that Eric wore, didn't appear to be functioning either. That hadn't stopped her from pushing all the buttons several times, hoping to recreate the same musical combination Eric had used, but the instrument made no sound.

Had the Councilman switched hers for a broken codex? Or were the thick prison walls preventing the codex from functioning? It had been a hellish couple of days, leaving no time to study the wrist units. She'd figured Eric could give her some one-on-one training in a week or two. When things had calmed down.

Not great planning on her part.

And if she couldn't use her stylus to draw her way out of here, or portal her way back through the codex's abilities, she was literally stuck here with only old fashioned methods of escape. Now if only she knew what they were.

With no weapons or anything to make a weapon from, it's a good thing she had yet to see her captors. For all intents and purposes, she'd been dumped into a hole in the ground and forgotten.

A horrible thought and one she really didn't want to dwell on.

If only she had her stylus. She could only hope whoever had it was taking care of it. There were souls in there. Souls that needed care.

Wait.

She had been able to communicate verbally with her stylus, at least while she'd been holding it. She'd still had to write the answers down, but…maybe she could scratch a message in the dirt? Their bond was strong and they would eventually be able to communicate telepathically – when her skills developed further.

It was worth a try. But what did she have to scratch in the dirt with? The tab on her jacket zipper caught her eye. Made from hard metal, it had ripped half off already. With a hard tug, she pulled the tab off. Walking back to where she'd first regained consciousness, she squatted and scratched in the ground, *Stylus, can you hear me?*

Silence.

Pressing harder, she scratched again. *Stylus, I'm in trouble. Can you help?*

More silence.

Damn it. Fear started an insidious slide inside her mind. She tried again, harder, almost making her fingers bleed with the attempt. *Stylus. I need help. Contact Paxton. I need Eric's help to escape.*

Nothing.

What had she expected? She bowed her head.

Essentially, she'd been tossed into a hellhole and no one knew. Except…maybe the Councilman. The man was a power hungry toad. Remembering the look of satisfaction in his beady eyes as she disappeared to God knew where sent more shivers down her spine. It also had another effect.

Anger and pride rose to battle the loneliness and fear. She would not let him win.

She refused.

PAXTON LET HIS stylus move freely across the page. Eric crowded behind him, trying to read the message as it came through.

Storey is calling for help.

Both men gasped. Paxton quickly scratched out a question. "Where is she?"

Not here.

"We know that. Is she at her home?" Eric snapped, worry making his voice sharper than he intended.

No.

Paxton frowned. "Is she in her home dimension?"

No.

Horror rose in Eric's stomach and was matched by the horror in Paxton's eyes. "Do you know where she is?"

No.

"Then how did you know to contact us?"

Her stylus says she is trying to contact Eric.

Excitement whistled through Eric. He knew Storey would find a way to contact him. They'd rescue her yet. "Why can't her stylus bring her home?"

Silence.

With growing unease, Eric said to Paxton, "Ask if Storey has her stylus with her."

Eyes wide, Paxton did as requested. The answer wasn't

long in coming.

No.

Both men shook their heads. Eric frowned, trying to figure out how this communication worked. "Then how did the stylus know that Storey is trying to contact us?"

Paxton's jumped in with another question first. "So Storey can communicate with her stylus, even though she's not touching it?"

With the souls in it.

Both men cried out in unison. "Soul bound."

Paxton then asked, "Then where is Storey's stylus?"

We don't know.

Eric pushed forward with the questions. "But you can communicate with it, correct?"

Yes.

"Then where is it?"

It doesn't know.

"Is it in this dimension?"

No.

"Is it in Storey's dimension?"

No.

The questioning continued until they determined that the stylus was in the same dimension as Storey, but not close to her. Close enough for her to communicate with it, but not close enough for her to see or touch it.

Eric ran his fingers through his hair. "Well, thank heavens for that. I was afraid she'd lost the stylus somehow. How long before their separation affects Storey's health?"

Paxton raised his gaze to Eric's. He frowned, intense worry developing in his eyes. "I don't know. That's why we didn't take it from her when she was first here, remember."

Eric straightened. "I thought I saw the Councilman with

a stylus in his hand. I wondered at the time…but there's been so much going on, I didn't think about it any further."

"My stylus said it isn't here, remember." Paxton watched him. "But they are valuable. Priceless in fact." His voice lowered. "If he has one, I need to see it."

Eric's mind locked onto the memory of Storey creating a dummy stylus. *Could that possibly be the one his father had? Really?*

Storey might have let down her guard in the celebratory atmosphere after the battle, but she was pretty cagey. She'd have kept a firm grip on her real stylus.

He closed his eyes briefly, and bit back the curses that threatened to pour from his lips. Another side effect of having Storey in his life, no matter how briefly. People in his dimension didn't swear. It was considered a grave insult and showed a complete lack of respect to the person being spoken to. Unfortunately swearing appeared to be a natural part of her upbringing.

"Eric? What's the matter?"

Eric turned to look at his mentor. Paxton had been horrified by Storey initially, but had come to respect what she'd been capable of doing. After all, it was because of her they'd won the war. So fast and so efficiently, it had been a non-war, really.

"I'm remembering something Storey did when we were on her side of the veil. Using the stylus she created a copy of it, hoping the duplicate might fool the Torans who'd planned to separate it from her."

Paxton's mouth dropped then slowly closed as he processed the concept. "Did it work?"

Not knowing exactly what 'it' referred to here, Eric clarified. "The new stylus appeared to be identical but when she tested it, it didn't work. I'm not sure if we ever asked the stylus why, but we assumed at the time it was a dud. Although Storey wondered if it didn't work because it had no souls bound to it."

Paxton's face shifted and changed with understanding, finally coming to rest with a reflection of wonder. "How could she even think to try such a thing?"

Eric grinned. "That's the joy of Storey. The way she thinks and processes problems and solutions is so different from us. It makes her ideas seem radical."

Paxton walked over to where the Councilman had been sitting. "He can't have a real one because your stylus said it wasn't here. Therefore he has to have the fake one, but *thinks* he has the real one."

The two stared at each other, letting the issues settle in.

Eric groaned. "Do we know if we can send messages back? We need to find her."

"I don't think so, because she hasn't got her stylus to receive the messages." Paxton pulled gently on his long white beard. "Although we can't underestimate her."

"Let's try to reach her anyway." Doing anything was better than doing nothing.

Paxton grabbed his writing tablet. "And let's see if we can find that empty stylus."

CHAPTER 3

STOREY SAT BACK on the dirt and wondered what else she could do. She needed her stylus. Holding her zipper pull, she started scratching again. "Stylus, can you come to me?"

Her hand jerked.

No.

Storey gasped in joy. It was here! And responding to her. Excitedly she tried to marshal her thoughts and figure out her next questions in some kind of coherent manner. "Stylus, are you being held by another person?"

No.

"Stylus, are you close to me?"

Yes.

Yes. But not in this prison as far as she could tell. So the odds were good her captors, whoever they were, had her stylus and paper. "Stylus, has anyone attempted to use you yet?"

No.

"Do the people who separated you from me understand what you are?"

No answer.

Of course there was no answer. How would the stylus know what her captors understood and what they didn't? This wasn't getting her anywhere.

She also needed a washroom and couldn't see any such facility here. In fact, she couldn't see much at all. The lighting was unique. Cool, but definitely weird. Still, it helped to keep back the chilling fear that the darkness let in so easily.

Now if only she could get the hell away from here before her captors returned. On the heels of that thought came the next pressing fear.

What if no one ever came?

WITH PAXTON CONTINUING to send messages to Storey's stylus, and hopefully to Storey herself, Eric decided to double check she hadn't made it home first, then gotten into trouble. Just to make sure. With Paxton guarding the lab, Eric crossed into Storey's dimension.

Opening his eyes on the other side, he realized the codex had sent him back to Bankhead mine where Storey had first crossed into his world. He retraced the well-traveled route back to Storey's two-story clapboard house. Approaching from behind, he checked out the back of her house. He couldn't see any sign that the Louers had ever been here. Had it only been days since they'd tried to tear through the dimensional fabric beside Storey's portal?

The lights were off in the house. Could he port into her bedroom? His codex had taken him there several times, so in theory, it should have the destination in its memory banks.

Punching the instructions into his wrist unit, he then waited for the black mist to wrap around his legs and transport him to her room. Thankfully, the darkness covered his actions in case any of the neighbors spotted him outside. The smoke dissipated quickly. Relieved, he noted the same childish posters on the walls and everything else that made a typical Storey looking bedroom. In fact, it didn't look any different than when he'd last seen it.

Not true. There was one big difference. Storey wasn't in it.

Hearing noises in the hallway, he quickly stuffed himself into her closet, overwhelmingly packed with years' worth of clothes and stuffed animals. And sketchbooks. Would any have her sketched portals? They'd come in handy to rescue her.

The sounds approached. Damn. He hoped it was Storey.

Just then the door pushed open and heavy footsteps sounded. A male voice muttered, "Damn lights. When are they going to come back on?"

"Storey? Are you in here?" The footsteps crossed the floor to Storey's bedside. "There's no sign of her."

"Are you sure? Oh dear." Storey's mother, at least he thought it was Storey's mother, stood just inside the room, enough that she could see the empty bed herself. "Where could she be?"

"Storey has never done anything rebellious up to now so maybe we're overreacting. What's the chance she's in the den like we found her last night?"

"Oh, I hope so. She's probably fallen asleep again with her drawings."

The lighter footsteps rapidly exited the room and headed down the hallway. The heavier footsteps followed.

Eric had his answer. Storey never made it home.

Damn. That meant she'd gone missing from his dimension.

STOREY'S NEED TO find a washroom had gone way beyond bad. When she had no other options, she had no qualms about going outdoors. But this prison was hardly outdoors. It also didn't offer toilet paper. She frowned and dug through her pockets. Tissues, three of them, lay crumpled at the bottom of her hoodie pocket. So that problem was solved, at least this time, but location wise, no. Nor did she have any idea if she was being watched. That possibility creeped her out.

She got up and wandered the large space for what had to be the umpteenth time. The light went on and off with her voice. She'd tried to order food and water the same way, with no luck. That there were no bodies gave her hope that she hadn't been dumped and left forever. Still, how long were they planning on leaving her here?

"Damn, why is there no door? There has to be a way in and out." The voice-activated lights meant someone had been here at one time. The concept of a door wasn't too outrageous.

"If there is a door, where the hell is it and why won't it open on command?" *Or had it?* Could it have opened silently? She might have missed it in the shadows. Anything was possible. With her hand in constant contact of the wall, Storey circled the room until she came to an open space. *A doorway.*

Was it a trap? It didn't really matter. She had to try to escape. With a deep breath, she snuck up to the door-way…then bolted through.

But to what?

More darkness. She couldn't see a thing. A round, metal, hand-sized button sat barely visible on the wall beside her. She slapped her hand on it. The door closed softly behind her.

Weird. Opened by voice and by hand. Double weird.

"Thank heavens for that," she muttered. "Now if only there were lights on."

Instantly the space lit up.

"Right. Voice controlled." Storey felt like an idiot. But a quick scan showed this smaller anteroom was also empty. The only sign of another possible door was a second metal button on the far wall. Checking that there was nothing usable in the room she dashed to the button and slapped it. "Lights off," she added, not wanting anyone who might be on the other side to see her.

Although if they lived in this type of natural darkness, their vision had to be better than hers.

The door opened, smoother this time, and quieter. The doors were some sort of stone or compressed sand. Adobe maybe. She didn't know. It was definitely odd.

The next room had more lights, giving her a dim view of odd shapes.

Still, a pervading silence filled the air. Did no one speak? No music? Television? Thinking back, even the Louers she'd seen in the attack had been silent.

Yet the lights were voice, sound or movement activated. Odd.

Taking a chance, she whispered, "Lights on half."

The lights pulsed on, dimmer this time, like fluorescent bulbs; chunks of luminosity lined the corner of the ceiling and shone on another large and empty room. So where the hell was everyone? Not that she wanted to see them, but she wanted to avoid a room full of them.

"Stylus, where are you?"

Not like it could answer her. Yet, she felt it. Sensed it

trying to speak with her. A quick look around showed no stylus or paper. Everything appeared to have been formed from the same odd rock.

She could use her zipper pull again, if she had no other options. She fished it out of her pocket and held it tightly. As a weapon it wasn't much either.

Carefully, she slipped along the closest wall, willing it to lead her to safety…and to her stylus.

How was it she hadn't become sick without it? Or was it still close enough that she hadn't experienced any harm yet?

The wall went on forever. What an odd formation. Molded lumps rose from the middle of the floor as if they were furniture of some sort. Maybe this was a meeting area.

She tried to stay clear of the lumps. There's no way she wanted a repeat of her experience in Paxton's apartment where the furniture had shifted in its attempt to fit whatever sized person it needed to. Who knew what the furniture here could do? It might be made of natural materials, but that didn't stop things from doing weird stuff.

From the smell and the darkness, she'd assumed she was in the Louers' dimension. And if the Louers had already migrated to the new dimension, this one could theoretically, be empty. She brightened at that thought. Except they hadn't had time to migrate a whole species to the new dimension she'd created for them. Then again, there were only thousands of people here, not billions like in her dimension.

She couldn't imagine trying to move her people to an-other place. War would break out on a half dozen fronts. The first country across would probably claim the entire dimension as their own.

What a disaster that would be. How long had it been

since she'd created that dimension? Hours or days. Had to be days. In the murky shadows, time had so little meaning. There were no sunrises or sunsets, no moon phases, nothing.

Storey closed her eyes and concentrated hard on connecting with the stylus. She could almost feel it. It was so vague, just a sensation really. She slid along the wall for another good fifty feet.

Where the hell was she?

ERIC CLOSED HIS eyes as the footsteps disappeared back downstairs. If those had been Storey's parents – a big maybe, because he remembered her saying she hadn't seen her father in over ten years – then something had gone majorly wrong in her dimension.

Vaguely he remembered her saying something about her family and how messed up things had become. If that man wasn't her father, then who was he and did it matter? Eric didn't want to deal with an angry male. Humans were more aggressive than his people. The Torans had evolved differently, choosing to use their psychic energy more, and had developed skills that were far superior to individuals in Storey's world. But his people weren't fighters.

Humans, on the other hand, had developed into warmongers. That's why the possibility of war on his side had stunned his people. They'd had no exposure to such violence. Only Storey hadn't been paralyzed. And she'd saved them all.

Now she was the one in need of saving.

CHAPTER 4

S TOREY CREPT AROUND another corner. Her mouth was so dry with fear she could barely swallow.

The silence unnerved her just as badly as if she heard the sound of footsteps.

Either this place was deserted or the Louers were professionals at staying quiet.

What about children? Did they have any here? Or were they in a different location? Not that she'd expect children close to a prison. Then again, she had so little information she couldn't afford to make any assumption. For all she knew, the Louers were herding her in a specific direction – like a trap.

Taking a deep breath, she rounded another corner, her back sliding along the wall. More blank walls faced her. She'd do a lot for a map of this place. Actually she'd do damn near anything to get her hands on her stylus.

A horrible sense of loss built deep inside her. The feeling so strong she had to consider that the stylus might be moving further away from her. It felt that bad. The nausea in her stomach made her want to heave. Yet, she didn't dare think that way. She had to find it. And fast.

Then the truth hit her, freezing her body in place. *Shit.*

The stylus hadn't moved – she had. In the wrong direction.

Crap. She really didn't want to go back, but the stylus was her only hope of getting out of here. There was no choice. How could she pinpoint its location? Especially when the stylus couldn't tell her.

Either way the problem wasn't going to solve itself while she sat paralyzed with indecision.

Damn it.

She'd been communicating with the stylus somewhat. At least enough to kinda feel the answers to her questions. Could she do a hot and cold thing, like that children's game?

But she'd have to get a lot closer to test the idea out.

Groaning silently, she headed back to the entrance of the room she'd woken up in. The journey only took a few minutes. Her body didn't care; her heart had started pounding with the first step and her palms had to be leaving sweat marks. She could probably turn the lights on, but that didn't guarantee success at this point and would alert everyone as to where she was. Not that any Louers had come after her yet. And that didn't make sense either.

That just brought her back to the whole trap concept. Not her favorite one to dwell on.

The only sound was her heavy, rasping breaths. Damn. She'd never hear the stylus with that interfering. She took a deep breath and released it. Then did it again. That helped.

A bit.

At the entrance to the huge room, she peered around the doorway. Her eyes adjusted slowly to the deep darkness.

Still empty and open. That wouldn't be the most brilliant engineering she'd seen. Then again, just how far behind were these people? And yes, they were people, as much as it was hard to claim them as a relative of her own kind. The Torans, Eric's people, had developed more psychically than her own. Whatever that meant. It's not like she'd seen any examples of that.

Her people had developed differently as well. So in theory, the Louers could be more intelligent, more advanced than either humans or Torans. Or they could be the very opposite. Their living hadn't been the easiest but they had survived. Survival meant development of some kind.

She slipped past the door and headed the way she should have when she first escaped.

"Stylus, are you there?"

The faint sensation was a warm buzz in her head.

Thank God for that.

More confident now, she picked up the pace, trying to follow the warmth or coolness of the buzz as a directional signal. It grew stronger and stronger. A comforting sense of companionship. She wasn't alone. The stylus was here. Waiting for her.

Moving as fast as she could in the darkness, she passed a series of doors. Probably doors as each had a silver disc or button. She could only hope they didn't have any Torans or humans locked up in any of those rooms or she'd have to try and get them out, too. Damn, she needed her stylus.

Tuning into the buzzing noise in her head, she blocked everything else out and focused on following it.

Several long minutes later, she had no idea where she was; so focused on making the buzzing in her head grow, she'd followed the wall to what appeared to the be the end of the road. Another wall stood in front of her.

Mentally, she tapped into the stylus. *Can you feel me, Stylus?*

Nothing.

Damn. She snatched up the metal zipper pull and asked

the question, this time she had her hand on the wall as it jerked with the answer. *Yes.*

Thank God for that. "Are you close to me?"

Yes.

And what did close mean? "Stylus, can you tell me the distance that's between us?"

Ten.

Ten what? Again, she had no idea of what measurements were used by Torans or Louers.

"Ten feet?" she asked cautiously.

Ten nacrons.

Shit.

"How long is a nacron?"

One nacron is ten sedents.

Double shit. Storey banged her forehead on the wall in front of her. Figures.

"Stylus, are there any Louers with you?"

No.

That was a relief.

"Are you contained in some way?"

Silence.

Stupid question, Storey. "Can you give me directions to find you?"

Follow the connection.

Connection? The buzz? Of course. That was how she'd made it this far, after all. She turned so her back pressed against the wall and closed her eyes. Where was the buzz coming from? The right. Great. That was the wall. No metal discs in sight.

"Stylus, I think you are behind the wall in front of me, but I can't see a way to get in."

Door.

"Yeah. That would be helpful." She thought hard. "Do they all have metal discs to show you how to open them?"

No.

Crap.

Backing up several steps, she took another look at the end wall. It made sense that there would be a way to open it, but how? The wall itself was about the length of her bedroom. And didn't that thought bring a pang to her heart? She missed her mom. That surprised her. But right now, a cup of tea with her mother sounded like the best gift ever.

Until she remembered that the last time she'd seen her mother, her father had been there, too. The same father she hadn't seen in a decade.

She shuddered. What a mess she had to clean up when she got home.

One mess at a time.

That meant getting out of here.

And that meant getting through the damn wall standing between her and her stylus.

Shit.

Taking several steps back, she ran, shoulder down, straight at the wall.

ERIC SLIPPED OUT of the closet and studied Storey's bedroom. Surely if she'd been back there'd be a sign. Like her backpack, sketchbook or even her shoes could be here. Something would have been disturbed. The trouble was he couldn't tell.

From what he could see, she hadn't made it back to her home dimension. That matched the stylus's words and her parents' conversation. That left two more dimensions that he was aware of, both potentially full of the enemy.

Not good. He was very much afraid Storey was in the new dimension she'd created.

And if so, that could be a huge problem.

With a final look at her room, he set his codex for home and sent himself back to Paxton's lab.

Paxton waited for him as the mist dissipated. "Well," he asked impatiently, "Did she make it there?"

"No. I need to go to the new dimension. Make sure she hasn't somehow gotten into that one."

"Absolutely not. We can't have any energy moving between that dimension and ours. You know as well as I do that the more we travel the more the energy instinctively aligns into a pathway. If we go over there, the Louers could eventually find their way back here."

"If Storey is over there, we have to get her back."

"Go ask your father if he knows anything about her whereabouts."

Eric frowned at his mentor. "He's not likely to tell me, you know that." Paxton refused to meet his gaze. "You think she might be dead or at least dying, don't you?"

"It's a distinct possibility. Now hurry."

Eric strode down the long white hallway. It had taken Storey's comment about the white being everywhere to make him realize how odd his world must look to her. Her dimension swelled with color and chaos. Peace and quiet were hard to find, but the place buzzed with activity. At home, calm ruled and the most excitement on a normal day was watching the sun go down. Nothing ever happened – until Storey had popped in. She'd brought some of the same chaos and color to his world, too. He enjoyed the energy and he *really* missed the chaos.

Stupid.

He missed her even more.

His father's chambers lay at the end of the hall. As Councilman, his chambers were the largest and richest of any here. He was big on appearances. Not so big on sharing.

At a white door that looked the same as every other apartment on this floor, Eric took a deep breath, thought of Storey caught in a nightmare dimension, possibly dying, and knocked on his father's door. Hard.

The door opened under his hand. Eric entered expecting to see his father holding court with the other council members. The room was silent – and empty.

Eric frowned. "Father. Are you home?"

"Father?"

No answer.

He called out again, moving cautiously into the open space. The room appeared to be undisturbed. But if he wasn't here, then where was he? His father only frequented a few places. Council Chambers, his apartment and Paxton's lab. The only other place would be the private dining room. But at this hour of the morning? Not likely.

His father was a creature of habit.

So where was he?

STOREY HIT THE wall and bounced off. *Duh.* Rubbing her sore shoulder she glowered at the dirt wall. "This is ridiculous. Why doesn't anything work properly around here?"

She walked back and forth along the wall with her hand scraping the surface, looking for some kind of crack or door; any weakness would be a good start. There had to be some way to get past this barrier. And fast. *Shit.*

At the far end she turned to look back along the wall. Nothing had changed.

"Open sesame?" Stupid, she knew it was stupid, but she was willing to try anything. Nothing happened. Of course not. Still, she had to try. "Door open?"

"Please open the door?"

Nothing happened.

Like who said the Louers even spoke English. For all she knew they had a very different language. Not that having another dialect would make any sense, considering the Toran people spoke a basic form of English. They had some words she'd never heard of. Still, it was close enough to hers to be understandable. Unlike their portal technology. That's what she really wanted to take home. *Like that will ever happen.* Still, imagine being able to go to California for a swim and Hong Kong for a shopping trip and then ending up in Paris for dinner. Travel by codex was fast and simple. It was also green technology. At least she thought it was. It would eliminate the need for planes, trains, cars even. The air would be almost pollution free. So much nicer than walking along the street with all the car exhaust she had to breathe in now.

Well not right now. Right now she was in the Louers' dimension. At least she thought she was. Then she could possibly be underground in the new dimension, too.

Let's face it. I have no clue where I am.

"Enough, already. Door open."

A grinding sound filled the area. The wall in front of her slid to the side. She pivoted, crouching low only to see she was still alone. Then she slipped into the room and stopped just inside the doorway. Was it the tone of voice that mattered here? Odd, considering she'd heard no sounds here.

In fact, the silence was starting to bug her.

"Lights on."

Instantly the same lighting system turned on, giving a low yellowish light over what appeared to be another empty room. "Crap. I like peace and quiet as much as the next person, but all the time? No. Are there any Torans here? Anything but Louers?" Silence was her only answer. Good thing, too, otherwise she'd have had a heart attack. "Stylus, are you in here?"

She didn't have her zipper tab in her hand. Damn. Digging deep, she scrounged around in her pockets until she found it. From what she could see, there was nothing in this room. Turning to the closest wall, she repeated the question, her hand ready to write the answer.

Only there was no answer.

Shit.

"Stylus? Stylus, talk to me."

No answer.

Double shit. It had been here a minute ago. She knew that. Had felt that deep connection, so close, and now it was gone. Where and how?

Closing her eyes, she called out as strongly as she could on a mental level.

No response.

Somehow, within the last five minutes, she'd lost her connection to the stylus. Why? Her heart raced. She walked the perimeter of the room looking for anything that would show storage, another door, Louers…something to explain how her stylus could have gone missing.

And came up empty.

"Stylus, do you have a power source that has run out? Like a battery or something?"

No answer.

Fear crept down her spine. All alone was one thing, all alone without the stylus was a whole different problem. Up until the last couple of minutes, she'd thought she was close to holding it again in her grasp.

Now what?

ERIC STOOD IN the middle of his father's chambers. Where was his father? Searching as he walked, Eric returned to Paxton. "My father isn't there. I can't find him anywhere."

Paxton lifted his head, concern clouding his eyes. "He can't be far. Everyone is still on alert. Just because the war is over doesn't mean the danger is."

Eric shrugged. "I couldn't find him. Ask your stylus."

Paxton frowned. "We can't be bothering it for every little thing. Walk the building and find him. He's probably in the dining room."

Studying his codex, Eric typed in a series of numbers to see if he could track his father. "I don't know. This doesn't feel right."

"Why?"

"The codex isn't picking up his wrist unit."

"I believe he has the broken one, remember? I tried to fix it, but he wanted it back before I completed the job." Paxton looked at the charts and papers covering his desk. Grabbing a blank page, he picked up his stylus. "Stylus, where is the Councilman?"

His hand jerked as the message came through. *Gone.*

"What does that mean?" Eric stared at the paper. "Gone where?"

"Stylus, has the Councilman left the building?"

Yes.

"There's no way. He almost never leaves. Ever." Eric glanced at Paxton, his uncertainty mirrored in his mentor's gaze.

Paxton shook his head. "That's not true. The Councilman prefers to stay inside, but he does leave when he has to."

"So where is he then?"

Turning back to the stylus, Paxton wrote, "Stylus, can you tell us where he has gone?"

No.

Paxton frowned. "No, you can't tell us or no, you can't tell us where he's gone?"

I don't know.

Both Paxton and Eric stared at each other in confusion. "I don't understand. Has something changed that you aren't getting the information you need?"

"Is it broken?" Eric figured to clear the air right away.

"No, at least I don't think so. Stylus, are you broken?"

No. Cloudy. Injured.

Paxton immediately laid it on top of the paper. "See, we probably overused it."

"No way. We have to figure out what's wrong. For all you know this is related to Storey's stylus. Maybe hers has been broken. They are all connected remember."

"I remember," he answered testily. "That's still a big assumption."

Eric tried to be patient. "I'm not assuming anything. I'm asking you to pick it up again and get more answers."

Paxton waffled then relented. He reached out for his stylus hesitantly. "I don't want to hurt it."

"Then ask it if you are doing anything to hurt it."

Paxton asked the question and his shoulders sagged with

relief when the answer came back 'no.'

"Now find out who's been injured," Eric urged.

The ensuing conversation blew him away. He'd been right. Something had happened to Storey's stylus and it had gone into sleep mode. Leaving her alone and probably in the Louers' dimension.

"Sleep mode?"

We turn off and hibernate after a long period of inactivity...or if someone happens to pick us up that we feel we are better off to hibernate from.

Eric didn't like the sound of that. "Can it tell if something happened to Storey?"

The answer came back negative. But that could mean it didn't know.

Shit. "I have to go find her. And her stylus apparently."

"I don't have a good feeling about this," Paxton said.

Eric's stomach twisted in agreement. "While I'm looking for Storey, maybe you can find my father."

Walking past Paxton's work desk, Eric snatched up a second codex for Storey, just in case. Last time he'd been in that horrible place, they hadn't had enough traveling power for everyone and that shortage had sent them into the newly created fourth dimension. Back then it had been empty. Now...it could be full of Louers. Securing the new codex to his right arm, he used the codes he'd thought to never repeat. The one difficult thing about codex travel, it needed coordinates. He'd only been in one place in that horrible land – a prison. Therefore, that's the only place he could return to.

As blackness swirled up around his body, he sent out a silent hope that he'd make it through this trip fine.

The last thing he wanted was to end up a prisoner – again.

CHAPTER 5

STOREY PRIDED HERSELF on staying calm and rational in difficult circumstances. She'd learned a lot through the skirmishes in Eric's dimension and knew she needed to control the panic crouching on the edge of her mind. The bottom line to her situation is she *had* to find her stylus. It had been elemental to every successful thing she'd done so far.

Why had it stopped communicating? Did it have batteries to run dry? Or, as it was bound to her, maybe it needed to spend time with her to recharge. With a few short steps, she returned to the wall she'd tried to bust through. She'd been so sure the stylus had been on the other side, and that's the last sensation she'd had of it, then it had stopped.

Cracks went up and down. Cupboards?

Could it be?

Quickly she searched for some way to open them. "Cupboards open." Nothing. *Crap, this again.* "Storage open. Door open. Wall open?"

Nothing.

She pounded along the crack, hoping it might have a release lever. Again nothing. The longer she stared at the wall the more she could make out the vertical lines that had to be there for a reason.

It had to be a cupboard of some kind. Organized cracks

filled the wall like the outline of a puzzle. It's like she looked at the backside of a storage unit.

That couldn't be right. On the other side she'd run her hand along the entire wall and there'd been no cracks or breaks at all. So between that wall and here, there had to be storage. And her stylus was in there. And if it was in there, someone had put it there. Now if only she knew who and how. Damn it.

With a heavy sigh, she reached up a hand and massaged her neck. Everything was starting to ache. And her stomach was growling from lack of food. Another growing problem. Food. And water. Damn, she shouldn't have thought of that, now her mouth was dry and all she could think of was cold, clear water. She closed her eyes and tried to focus. *Stylus? Please, are you there? I need to find you.*

Again, she heard nothing.

But…but what? A faint buzz, so faint she could almost persuade herself she'd imagined it. There it was again. With an ear cocked to one side, she walked toward the noise. It was coming from the corner of the wall. Reaching out, she touched the spot gently. Then harder. *Snick.* The cupboard in front of her opened up. She backed away. It didn't snap open or open by much, but it was as if some interior connection had released and there was now a big enough crack to pull the door toward her. She opened it, expecting to see shelves. Instead, a space, too big for the area she'd thought had been available for the cupboard stood in front of her. Big enough she could walk inside. And that thought made her stomach cringe. Because not only could she *not* find her stylus lying on the dirt floor of this cupboard, she also couldn't see a back to the cupboard. There wasn't one.

Because this wasn't a cupboard, but a doorway.

ERIC COUGHED, GASPED, then coughed again. The smell.

His eyes streamed and his chest burned. How could the Louers live with this stench? He coughed and coughed, almost retching as his system struggled to adapt. Bending over, he gave himself another long moment to adjust. The crossing had been easy enough, but the arrival had been tough.

Standing slowly, he searched the area around him. The darkness held a dense, cloying odor. He squinted. It appeared to be the same room he'd been in last time. It also appeared to be empty.

Relaxing slightly, he rolled his head and scrunched his shoulders slightly to ease up the tension in his back. He did a quick walk of the perimeter of the large room. No lights, no door, nothing. How did that work?

The Louers' technology had diversified from those of his own people centuries ago, so even though he might know some of their methods to make daily living work, chances are he wouldn't understand all of it. His father and Paxton assumed that the Louers had become even more primitive after they'd been banished to this hell, but he wasn't so sure. The two men held the same opinion of Storey and her people, and look at what she'd managed to do. If the Louers had developed half as well as the humans, they could have some pretty amazing technology.

The Louers he'd seen on his dimension had been brutish in looks, but they had been incredibly strong. They'd also crossed the veil and devised a strategy to try and take over his world. That they hadn't succeeded was due mostly to Storey and they couldn't have known to account for her in their plans. Who could have?

He grinned.

Good for Storey. Just being herself had been enough to make his people stand up and take notice. Teach them for acting superior and thinking all other people were inferior. He planned on not making the same mistake.

So…how to get out of here and find Storey?

With a hand held against the wall, he quickly searched for openings in the weird sandstone walls. Just because he couldn't see any light source didn't mean there wasn't one. Taking a chance on attracting attention, he called aloud for light. Instantly the room flooded with bright light. So they had that much. Great. Maybe this wouldn't be so hard after all.

"Door open."

Nothing.

Then again…

Using his best military sounding voice, Eric tried again. "Open prison door."

Nothing.

"Please open this door."

Nothing.

This was just going to make him mad. He'd assumed they had voice technology as his people did, so it made sense to have voice activated doors. However, if this was a prison then they wouldn't want the prisoners to get out, so chances were that the guards either had a voice print, word sequence or some other way of making sure only a select few people would be allowed to open the door. His people would do the same.

So back to Paxton's lab and see if his stylus would be able to get more information on the security here.

Frustrated, he tapped in the code to take him back to

Paxton's lab, the musical notes filling the large space. The echo was surprising but with so little ambient noise it reverberated around the room. As he readied to enter the last digit of the sequence, he heard a grating sound. Whirling around, he crouched, ready for an attack…and saw no one.

A huge door had opened. But no one came in. Were they waiting on the other side? He crept up behind the door and waited. Nothing. Peering through the crack between the door and the wall didn't help, only blackness showed on the other side. Of course the light was on his side. Taking a deep breath, he slipped out of the room and melted into the shadows on the other side. It took way too long for his eyes to adjust to the darkness. When they finally did, he found he was alone in another large, empty room.

Could the notes of his codex…have opened the door? That would mean they had music here. Or the door mechanism had been triggered by his movements. That didn't make sense either. Prisoners walked around all the time. The only other explanation he could imagine was a failsafe mechanism that opened automatically after a certain length of time. So that no one was left in there forever. That concept was kind of reassuring. But not much.

Choosing to go left, he crept down the hallway.

Storey was here somewhere.

STOREY STUDIED THE cupboard passageway. Dare she enter? How could she not?

Closing her eyes she called to the stylus.

The faintest of buzzes answered her. Shit. It was down here. The many thick walls might explain the stylus's inability to communicate. Could it die? Maybe it went to sleep or something until a new soul could bond to it. Maybe that's why it had bonded to her so strongly when she'd initially found it. So it would survive. In which case, what if it bonded with the Louer who'd found it here?

That wouldn't be good.

Decision made.

Focusing on the buzz, she strode into the dark tunnel. "Stylus, hold on. I'm coming. Stay strong. Stay connected."

A hum sounded. Stronger than before, but still indistinct. Even though she couldn't see what she walked on or anything two feet in front of her, she knew as strongly as she'd ever understood anything in her life, she needed to travel this pathway to her stylus.

She could only hope she'd find it in time to save them both.

Picking up the pace, she trotted down the corridor.

The end of the road came up and smacked her in the face – hard. She tumbled backwards. "Damn." Sitting up she rubbed her head and right elbow, sore from cracking hard on the ground. Getting up slowly, she put out a hand to touch the wall or door in front of her. "Door open."

Silently, the door moved toward her, forcing her back. The stream of light widened. An odd shuffling sound came through, soft and gentle, but unidentifiable.

Was there someone in the next room?

She closed her eyes and tried to control her gasping breath. The last thing she needed was for them to hear her. On the other hand, if they had her stylus and thought they were going to keep it, they had better think again.

So not going to happen. Not here. Her mother would be devastated at never knowing what had happened. Chances were good that Storey would become just another runaway teenager that was never heard from again.

Peering around the corner of the doorway, she realized she'd reached a small anteroom. Maybe it would be a sitting room off a bedroom in her dimension. Another weird table sat off to one side covered in items she couldn't decipher. Almost everything had a neutral color to it. The sheer drabness of this world hurt her creative soul, her artist soul. Where were the reds, greens and blues?

Very odd. She quickly scanned the room. It was empty. But there was an open doorway ahead of her. Maybe the person had gone into there.

She crept over to the table, ducking out of sight at the slightest sound. Lifting her head slightly, she checked to see if she was still alone.

Yes. She reached up to the stack of items on the table and picked up one for a closer look. It seemed somewhat like a cup, except too big for her small fingers to hold comfortably. The next item appeared to be made of the same material, almost a thin sandstone slice. It resembled a tiny box of some kind. It was also empty.

Weird materials.

Weird items.

Weird place.

The items were odd sized, too. The table was higher than she was used to; not that she had to stand on tiptoes to look down on it but she'd have a hard time doing any work on it comfortably. What's the chance her stylus was in the jumble? She didn't recognize it. And she didn't want to move around too much and alert whoever was in the next room. Hunkering back down, she searched the area again, and spotted another wall of cupboards like the last one she'd entered. And this one was open showing shelves on the one side. Closing her eyes she called out to the stylus in a soft whisper, "Are you there?"

A buzz answered her. Stronger, clearer, but still indistinct because she had no way to write the answers. She grabbed her zipper pull and held it against what must be a seat butted up against the side of the table and asked again.

Slowly her hand moved. *Yes.*

Oh thank heavens for that.

"Where are you?"

Don't know.

Of course it didn't. Neither did she. But…it was a computer-like thingy so maybe it could send out a beacon. "Can you send out a signal, a noise to let me know where you are?"

Instantly, there was an odd ringtone going off in her head. Or in the air? No, surely not. She spun around looking for the source. There, in the cupboards. Within seconds, she'd raced toward the spot, scared to alert whoever was in the other room to her presence. There were deep shelves inside. She quickly searched them. The stylus just looked like an old carpenter's pencil. Dull and dark, it was hard to see in the dark.

The noise was definitely louder here. Excited, she dropped to her knees and checked the bottom spaces. The noise increased to almost deafening now. A good sign. The last few items were almost recognizable. A ball, maybe a bat? A bunch of toys like a ball on string or wire and a wooden post. Like a child's closet. Off to one side were tablets of some kind. Maybe for writing on, like miniature chalkboards. Even chalk would be a huge help. By the time she'd moved to the next cubby hole the music in her head changed from a weird ringtone to an almost soothing lullaby.

"Does that mean I'm almost there, Stylus?"

The lullaby increased in volume. It increased so much, she could hardly stand it. She shoved her hand into the jumbled mess and closed around a half dozen objects.

Something made her fingers tingle.

The lullaby came to a dead stop.

Warmth shot up her arm. She withdrew her handful until she could see what she'd snagged clearly.

Her stylus!

Joy shot through her. *Yes!*

And then she took another look and stopped. How could this be possible?

There, clutched in her fingers, were three pencils that could have all been styluses. And maybe they were? Who would have stashed these in here, lost and forgotten? These gems could have saved the Louers so much hardship?

They might *not* be styluses, but as she studied each one, the magical lettering shone on the side of each one. Unbelievable. Did they have souls attached to them too?

And if there were three, what was the chance there were more?

It was important to find every one. How she knew that, she didn't know. But she did. Tucking those three securely into her pocket, she dove into the bottom of the cupboard and sorted through the mess. And found two more. Unbelievable. Now she didn't dare leave any behind. There were people in there, after all.

Knowing she didn't have the time to spare, but unable to help herself, she went back for a third and final search, and found one really old looking stylus jammed into the joinery at the very back. Six styluses. Pulling back slightly, a wary eye to the open door, she moved over and checked every cupboard, as fast and as systematically as she could in order to not miss one. Ten panicked minutes later, she held a broken one in her hand. No others though. Now to safety.

She ran across the room and back into the open doorway from where she'd entered.

Just as she hit the safety of the darkness, she heard a loud grunt behind her.

Shit.

ERIC'S EYES FINALLY adjusted to the dark as he paced forward, instinct keeping him moving in the same direction. He almost sensed Storey up ahead. Many of his people had strong psychic powers. His society used healers in their hospitals and people with an affinity for plants and growing in the gardens and greenhouses. Those that had a specialty were given the means to develop it as far as they could.

To the best of his knowledge, he possessed a weird navigational sense. It allowed him to find his way home from most places and could move toward something even if he had no idea where it was.

Unfortunately, he'd had little chance to develop that sense. And as it wasn't one of the known talents, his ability hadn't been given much training time. He'd yet to even mention it to Storey. She'd find it fascinating he was sure. And unlike his father, he doubted she'd laugh at it.

So he couldn't heal sick people or tell the future or lift items with his mind, like some of his people could, but surely being good at geography and navigation had to count for something. Of course, that's why he'd been put into Ranger training.

Eric's codex lit up like a Christmas tree. "What the..."

He kept running while trying to understand the odd

number sequences and lights. Was someone trying to contact him? Or was someone trying to navigate toward his last known location? The codexes were capable of so much more than what they were commonly used for that he often forgot about their other capabilities. Still, not many people would know about those extras either…except Paxton.

Should he go back to the lab and check? Or could he remember how to send a coded message? Something he hadn't done since his training days. Neither could he tap in Toranee code while running. Toranee was old in his world, and similar in some ways to the Morse code of Storey's dimension.

He wondered if one had spawned the other? Another piece of information his people had taken from her dimension?

That made it one of the more basic languages. And he couldn't remember much of it. Breathing hard, he came to a stop and crouched down out of sight. He lowered the volume on his unit and struggled to tap out a simple message to Paxton. It took several tries and head bangs, as Storey would say, to get out a quick note.

In Louers' world. On Storey's trail. Can't come back. Problems.

Eric sent it, hoping the last word would be understood. Then, hating the time he'd lost, he returned to trotting down the corridor. Storey was up ahead. Somewhere.

He had yet to see any Louers here, and that didn't feel right either. Surely they hadn't managed a complete migration already. They'd need time to move everyone and everything over.

Cold seeped into his arms and legs, even with the energy he was expending. The dark and the dirt, the smell and the cold, all combined to make this a very unwelcoming place.

Quite similar to Storey's first foray into his world actually. She'd landed in a big cave, a major crossing his people used regularly to move through dimensions and across his world. The crossing would have looked similar to what he'd seen here. Dirt walls, a room that went on seemingly forever — and all without seeing a soul.

Maybe this was a similar type of place in the Louer world. It's not like he'd had a chance to explore to know for sure.

His respect for Storey zoomed up another notch.

Now if he could just find her.

CHAPTER 6

S TOREY BOLTED THROUGH the dark tunnel, terrified she'd trip and drop the styluses. In her mind, she knew they could be just empty shells, but the personal connection to *her* stylus was real and precious. How could she desert the others – just in case?

She glanced behind her, scared she was being followed. Which didn't appear to be the case. Her footsteps slowed as she approached the next room. Why not?

Maybe they didn't mean her any harm.

Shit. She hated it when her softer side came out. For all she knew this was the last Louer here. Damn it. How bad could they be? They'd kept styluses and kids' toys. Kids' toys.

Her stomach twisted. What if that had been a child? A Louer child. Were there such things? Of course. They were people. Just a different kind.

If there was a child, was there an adult with it? Or had the child been left behind alone? By accident or on purpose?

With a heavy sigh, she realized she couldn't leave without knowing. Who knew if there was anyone left here to help them out?

Too bad all the styluses she'd picked up couldn't help. She held them gently in her hand. No heat emanated from them, like Eric experienced when he'd held her stylus. Would her stylus know if they were empty? Maybe. Now if only she had paper. The wall might work again, but something softer would be easier. Like her missing sketchbook.

With her stylus in her hand, she delighted when the sense of loss, of being alone, shifted to a full sense of connectedness. That instant knowing that this stylus was hers. Although identical in appearance to the others there was no doubt in her mind that she held her stylus. There was a link between them – strong, clearer than before. She didn't understand why. And didn't care.

"Stylus? Are you okay?"

She placed her stylus against the wall and read the faint impression in the dirt.

Yes. Getting stronger.

"Do you need much longer before you are back to full strength?"

No. Not long.

Whatever that meant in terms of time for a stylus. Rather than wasting time trying to sort it out, she asked if it had been a Louer who'd put the stylus in the closet.

There was a humming silence. *Yes. Almost.*

Storey paused, her mouth open. "Almost?" she asked cautiously.

Child.

Oh shit. "Oh no. We can't leave a child alone, can we?"

Yes, we can.

Of course the stylus didn't know about balancing morals and right and wrong actions.

"Is the child alone?"

Yes.

"How many Louers are there in this complex?" That wasn't quite the right word to describe this place, but it was all she could think of.

One. The child.

That finished it. There was no way Storey could leave without making sure the child would be okay. Louer or not, the child was alone. "How old is the child?"

She's six.

She? It was a little girl. Storey definitely wouldn't leave her behind, lost and alone. But… "Is she a danger to me?"

A humming sound filled the air. *No. We don't believe so.*

Believe? Storey would rather have a more definite answer than that. "Will I be able to communicate with her?"

Somewhat.

Sigh. Why was nothing ever easy? "Where is the child's family?"

In the new dimension.

Well that's good. At least she had a family. "Can we return the child to her family?"

Yes.

Thinking of the less than ideal lifestyle some kids in her human world experienced, she had to know. "Is she a wanted child? Or did they leave her behind on purpose?

Accident. Her pet ran away. She ran after it.

"Pet? I've yet to see anything living here. What type of pet?"

A skorl.

Yeah, that was so not helpful. "Did she find it?"

Yes.

"Can she take the pet with her to the other dimension?"

Yes.

"And no one has come back for her?"

They can't reopen the portal to come back.

Storey straightened as understanding swept through her. How sad. At the same time, she felt much better about not having to worry that she'd be recaptured. "Was she the one I saw on arrival?" It was getting easier to understand the stylus. Some of the words seemed to form in her mind. As if she were only partly reading and anticipating what the stylus planned to say before it actually did. Weird. But a relief. She'd take any improvement to her situation at this point.

She saw you arrive, thought you were her people coming back for her.

"So she left me there and took my stuff?" Storey didn't like the sound of that. Typical.

She thought you were dead.

"And where is my sketchbook?"

With the child.

"Why did she take you?"

She'd seen others like me.

"Does she know what you are?"

No.

"I found six of you in that cupboard. Are there more?"

A heavy humming filled the air. Then it was joined by a humming of a different tenor, then another and another. Pretty soon the air buzzed as if a conversation raced around her. They were styluses then.

No. You have us all.

"Should I leave any of you behind?"

No. We are grateful to you.

"What about the broken one?"

We are grateful that you picked up the broken one. He is an important member of our group.

"Can he be fixed?"

Yes.

Good enough. She tucked them all safely away in her pockets then returned to the problem of the Louer child.

"Stylus, can we write on her arm and send her to the new dimension like we did the prisoners from the war?

No.

She groaned. "Why not?"

I don't have the code for where her people are. If we sent her over she could end up anywhere.

Damn.

"So I'm all alone with a Louer child with no way to help either of us?"

Not quite.

Groaning a loud, she asked, "What's not quite right?"

You are not alone.

She spun around, searching for someone else to somehow, suddenly show up. "What do you mean? I thought you said the Louers were all gone except for the child?"

I did.

"So…"

A Toran is here now.

"Who?" But she knew. Only Eric would have come over and tried to help her.

Eric.

Yes! She turned around, listening for him. "Where is he?"

Not far.

"How far? Which way do I go to find him?"

You don't. He's following you.

"Perfect. So I can sit here and wait. Then he can help me deal with the issue of the child."

Yes.

A huge pressure valve inside eased. She wasn't alone. Thank God. "Stylus, are you okay now?"

Almost.

It had said that last time too. "What about the child, is she hurt?"

No. Hungry.

That figured. Weren't all kids? "Did the Louers get settled into their new dimension?"

In progress. The Louers of this complex moved, but the others haven't been able to yet. The portal is damaged. Closed.

Uh oh. That couldn't be good. Did the Louers even know the child had been left behind? And speaking of children and parents…

"Are my parents okay? Still together." Her question slid out, surprising her.

Yes.

"That's not good."

Why?

"My father hasn't been in my life for a long time. When I created the new dimension I did something to *my* dimension. My parents are different. Their beliefs are different. I'm supposed to be different. I asked you to reverse what I did, but I don't think you changed everything back." She hesitated. "Did you?"

No. Your words and thoughts weren't as one. You twisted time.

"Yeah, that doesn't sound so good. Can I untwist it? Or twist it back again?

No.

She took a deep breath. "Why? I need to reverse what I did to my dimension without affecting the other good changes I made."

You can fix this.

She breathed a deep sigh of relief. Thank heavens for that. "Now if only Eric would show up, things would be great."

He's almost here.

Storey turned to face the door. Wouldn't he get a surprise when he saw what she'd found.

ERIC FOLLOWED THE wall deeper into the Louers' complex, wondering at the weird sounds coming from his codex. Was it broken? Maybe the Louers' dimension was the problem.

The light on his codex changed. And a series of symbols sat in the small display window. Mentally he converted it to something understandable. Storey. He came to a sliding stop.

Her presence was stronger than ever. And close.

Did he dare call for her?

If any Louers were here, he should have seen some sign or them by now. He'd almost have preferred it. This lonely darkness was unsettling. As was the constant looking over his shoulder only to find nothing, anywhere.

"Storey," he whispered, then shook his head. How stupid. It's not like Storey could've heard that. She'd have to be right in front of him to hear him.

"Yes?"

Storey's pale face flashed in front of him, a huge grin and sheer joy in her eyes. "Did you call?"

"Storey!" he shouted, and snatched her up into his arms. He twirled her around, holding her close. *Oh, thank you!*

"Finally! I've been so worried." With a big grin he put her down then pushed her hair back so she could look into her face. He stared deep into her eyes. "What the heck happened? How did you end up here? Why couldn't you lcave?"

She laughed and jumped back into his arms. He held her tight, dropping his head to rest on hers. Joy rippled through him, so grateful to have her safe.

Finally she stepped back, her smile this time a little teary eyed. She sniffled and wiped her eyes. "Am I glad to see you." In a surprise move, she reached up and hit his shoulder. "That's for your lousy father." To be fair, as she had no proof, she added with a sigh, "At least I think this mess is his fault."

"I'm afraid it is too, but I don't have any proof yet." Eric bit back a sigh. He hoped his father was innocent. Except that concept was getting harder to believe. His father had to have been behind it. There'd been no one else with the motive, means and skill level to send Storey somewhere else. "You didn't even make it to your home, did you?"

"No. As I left the party, your father waved at me. In his hand he had my stylus. At least what he thought was my stylus. Oh, he gloated like he knew something bad was going to happen – something I was *not* going to like. And he was right." Storey shook her head at the memory. "When the mist dissipated, there were these horrible hands reaching for me. I don't know if it was crossing the dimension or what but I blacked out. When I came to, I was alone in a large cave-like room."

Eric closed his eyes. Damn. His father couldn't have known about her fake stylus. He'd intended to separate Storey from her stylus, thus bringing about her death. Could he have also changed the destination in her codex? Did he even know how to do that? The one was bad enough, but if he'd done them both…well, Eric didn't know what to think.

Could his father hate Storey that much? Or was this a desperate act of a desperate man? Could he have thought this was a way to regain his all powerful leadership status – using her as an example to others, perhaps? He'd never had to deal with outright defiance or a potential non-confidence vote before – until Storey. Could this be just about ego?

Or maybe fear was the basis of his father's actions. Fear of losing everything he had? Eric had heard mutterings from several displeased council members and presumed his father had as well. Would that have been enough to precipitate these actions?

Eric would have to let this mess roll around in his head for a bit.

Right now he had bigger priorities – like getting Storey home safely.

"It's going to be fine now. I have my codex and I brought another one for you." By the time he'd finished speaking, Eric had unclipped the spare on his left and snagged her arm to clip it onto hers.

He stopped. "What's this?"

"What's what?"

Eric tapped her arm.

"I can't see."

"Lights on full." Instantly the lights turned on, giving Storey her first real look at the large room. She couldn't believe the enormity of the space they were in. There had to have been many Louers living here to require a room of such size. It was bigger than the community center she'd gone to at home. "Wow. Look at this place."

"Wow," Eric said patiently, "Look at your arm." He grabbed her left arm and gave it a good shake.

Staring, Storey frowned at the intricate swirls decorating her arm. They traveled from the back of her wrist to her elbow and around the underside. She felt nothing as she ran her fingers over it. There was no burning, scarring or even loose ink to come off on her fingers.

"I have no idea. I don't know when or how I got these."

"It's also not *on* you; it's a part *of* you. Your people have tattoos inked into their skin. These are considered marks of honor in my home. I have no idea if the Louers have something similar in theirs."

"Marks of honor." She snorted. They were pretty cool looking. "That might have made sense if your people had given them to me on the night of the celebration. But not here and now. My arm was clean when I left your place."

"Somehow you've gained these marks in the time you've been here." He studied her face carefully, a hint of humor in his eyes. "You are the strangest girl."

"Oh," she gasped, "that is so unfair."

He grinned. "Only you could be banished to another dimension and come out with marks of honor without having any idea of how you got them."

She snickered. "I found a few other things here too." All humor fell away. Storey looked into his eyes, willing him to understand. "A lost Louer child for one. A little girl was accidentally left behind in the mass exodus of her people. According to my stylus there's something wrong with the portal and the Louers can't come back for her. She's all alone."

"What? A single juvenile? Oh, that's not good."

Storey nodded emphatically. "Exactly. I'm glad you understand. So, you'll help, right?"

Eric tried to figure out where Storey's lightning quick mind was going. A Louer child alone probably wouldn't survive and as much as he didn't like the idea, it might be a kindness to kill her now and prevent her suffering. But from the hope on Storey's face, he highly doubted he was going to like her solution.

"Help you do what?" he asked warily. Somehow he didn't think he was going to like her answer.

"Help me return her to her parents. In the new dimension."

Oh shit.

STOREY COULDN'T BELIEVE Eric stood in front of her. Only now that she realized she'd been saved, did she admit to herself how worried she'd been. How alone – how lost – she'd felt. Eric had become such a great friend with the potential to become so much more.

Unable to help herself, she reached out and hugged him again. As his arms closed around her, she finally realized he wasn't warming to her idea regarding the child. "Eric?"

"Hmmm." His husky voice against her ear melted her insides. Damn it was wonderful to have him here.

She pulled back slightly to see his expression clearer. "You don't think we should help her?"

"Have you seen her? Do you know how old she is? Can you talk to her?"

"According to the stylus, she's six." Storey frowned. Whatever that number meant to the Louers. "We can't just leave her. She'll die." She watched his conscience war with his upbringing. At least that's what she thought the fight going on behind his eyes was all about. The Louers were hated enemies of the Torans. It was natural for him to be concerned. But a child was a child regardless of her family. They had to help her. That was not negotiable.

What form that help took was up for discussion. "Can

we pinpoint where the Louers are in the new dimension and send her to them?"

Eric frowned.

She grinned at his automatic reaction to something he wasn't sure about. But his morals were good and his common sense sound. He'd come around and probably with a better idea than she had.

"I don't know how to do that," he said. "Paxton or your stylus might though. The first thing we have to do is find a way to talk to the child. If she doesn't want to come willingly, it's not going to be fun for any of us."

He had a point. Storey turned back to the room with the cupboard-door-looking hallway.

"There's a weird hallway in this room. I think she's at the far end."

"Show me."

Storey led the way back into the passageway. At the other end, it appeared as if the light was still on. There was no sign of the child in the first room. She motioned at the lit room ahead, then they walked quietly over to see if the child was in the second area.

The room appeared to be more of a bedroom than anything else Storey had seen in the place, but it didn't make much sense in layout. There were shapes similar to beds, but wider and shorter and they were stacked liked bunks. There was no bedding. Storey guessed everything necessary had been stripped. Since the Louers hadn't had much time for crossing over, it made sense that some belongings had been left behind for another trip. Although from what she could see, they'd done a decent job the first time around.

As she walked into the center of the room, she turned slowly, searching for the child. And found her backpack.

Yes. The bag sat on the floor, open and dumped. Even from where she stood, Storey could see the granola had been flattened. "I need to get my stuff," she whispered, nudging Eric's arm, she pointed to her bag. With a cautious look around, she raced forward and quickly grabbed up the remaining contents. Her sketchbook was missing. Figured.

Still no sign of the child. Or another door, either. Weird. Then again, what did she know about the doors here? They seemed to just appear. "Eric, I don't know where she is."

"Hiding most likely. It's what I'd do. Is everything here made of rock?" He walked over to the closest bed like structure and pushed down. "Looks like it."

"I wondered too. It looks like they've taken absolutely everything they could with them. Well, not quite. There are cupboards in the other room with some weird stuff left behind." Storey paused and spun around to face him, delight spreading across her face, as she remembered what else she'd found. "Guess what? I found more styluses. Six in all, including a broken one."

Eric spun so fast he almost knocked her over. "What? You found styluses? Like *our* styluses? Here? How?"

She pulled out two from her pocket. His look of astonishment grew. Flashing a big grin at him, she then tucked the items safely back away.

"Come. I'll show you." Storey led the way back through the tunnel. Inside the dark room again, she pointed to the shelves on the side. "They were tossed in there. I presume the child found mine in my backpack, recognized it and threw it in there with the others."

"Lights on." Instantly light filled the space.

Eric stared from her to the cupboard and back again.

"Chances are that if they've been here all this time, they won't work now."

"Maybe." Storey bent to look, yet again, into the back of the cupboard. And found herself staring into a pair of eyes.

She screamed and jumped back, her hand to her throat. "Good God. What is that thing? A rat?"

Eric leaned over to take a look. And grinned. "I think it's a skorl. We have them at home, but they've almost become extinct."

Storey took another look. The animal's small, beady eyes were set wide apart with a small nose. The rest of the rodent-sized critter appeared to be covered in a large amount of dust covered fur. It held out a paw, the fur stopping before switching to brown skin covered digits.

"That's the girl's pet, then," Storey said. "According to my stylus, when everyone was moving to the new dimension, her pet was scared off and she ran after him and got left behind. Now with the portal the way it is…"

Eric looked from her to the animal. "Don't tell me. We're going to have to save the pet, too?"

She grinned. "I knew you'd understand."

The small rodent with the big eyes sat on its haunches to stare at them curiously.

"I wonder if it bites?" he muttered.

"Probably," she said cheerfully. "It doesn't know you. If we could find the girl, she could retrieve it. Too bad they don't have a cage to carry it. I've never seen such a pile of junk." She pointed to the remaining contents of the cupboard.

Eric studied the almost empty shelves. "Think about it. They left behind…"

"…everything what wasn't needed or useable." Storey

finished.

"Exactly. They might have more things stored in another location to collect later. If the portal is damaged, maybe they haven't had a chance yet?" He cast another quick look around. "At least we know this group made it over to the new dimension."

"How do we get the pet out safely?" She bent again to take a cautious glance at the animal still sitting at the back of the cupboard. "It's liable to make a run for it if we try to capture it."

Eric sighed. "I really don't want to stick my hand in there and grab it. That thing is likely to take my fingers off."

"True." Storey grinned at the disgusted look on his face. "Do you think we should take the two of them back to your dimension first? Then figure out how to get her home to her family?"

He looked up at her from his squatting position. "Paxton would be horrified. Besides, you're making a big assumption here. We might not be taking her anywhere."

Storey refused to be put off. They'd faced much bigger obstacles and overcome them; this was no different. "Any better suggestions? We have to create a game plan. And to see if these styluses are okay. They're in hibernation, according to my stylus."

"You could contact Paxton and ask for advice. I'd hate to bring these two back unannounced."

"Except that I can't communicate very well with it." The backpack had been emptied. "No sketchbook, no paper. I can ask questions and he tries to answer, but sorting out what I'm writing on a wall in the dark isn't easy. And he's not back to full strength, although I'm not sure just what that means."

Eric stood up suddenly and reached into his back pocket. He pulled out two folded pieces of paper. "I found these in your bedroom. Use them."

She opened the paper up to find the several of the first portals she'd created. It seemed so long ago, but it had been…what…only a few weeks? Her fist pumped into the air. "Yes! We could be home in minutes." Homesickness hit, draining the excitement from her system. "You went to my place? To try and find me?"

"Yes."

"How…" Unexpected tears threatened to clog her vision. She cleared her throat. "How was my mother?"

"I am not exactly sure." He stared at her thoughtfully. "They know you're missing, because they came into your room while I hid in the closet."

"They," she said, her heart sinking. "My father was there?'

"Yes."

"So, the stylus was right again," she muttered, pulling the stylus out of her pocket. "Stylus, are you back to full working power yet?"

She didn't need paper to see her hand outline *No* in the air. "Damn."

"What's that all about?"

"We were separated too long, so it went into sleep mode, power saver mode or something. Now that it's with me it's recharging – if that's the proper word for what it's doing – but it's not all there yet. I can ask questions, but I don't think he can reach Paxton yet. Every time I ask about how long, he just says soon."

Just then noises from inside the cupboard, followed by scurrying feet, had her jumping back and out of the way as the skorl raced out. Eric was faster. He scooped it up and tucked into the front of his coat.

The little creature struggled and squealed worse than a pig only in a much higher-pitched voice. The sound rose in volume like a damned siren. Storey clapped her hands over her ears. "Make it stop."

With a grimace, he said, "I don't know how." He looked around. "Find something to carry it in, will you?"

Storey raced to the cupboard. Surely there'd be a container of some kind.

The sound of running feet was her only warning, then Eric yelled, "Hey, stop that!"

Storey spun around to find the Louer child, at least she figured that's what it was, screaming at Eric and pounding on his chest.

And what a noise came out of her mouth. Storey had never heard anything like it. And didn't want to again. *Jesus.* The squealing skorl had nothing on her. "Eric. Give it to her. She thinks you're hurting it."

"What?"

Storey shook her head and raced over. Eric was getting pounded on from both sides. And getting madder by the minute. She couldn't blame him. Storey wrapped her arms securely around the child, who came up to her ribs, but was probably close to Storey in weight, and pulled her back off Eric. Then she clapped a hand over the child's mouth to try to stop the weird noise coming out of her mouth.

It helped, but only a little bit. "Eric, show her the pet. She needs to see that it is okay."

Eric rolled his eyes and reached inside his jacket for the squealing animal. As soon as the skorl saw the child and the child saw her pet, they both shut up. The child put out her arms and Eric placed the animal in them. The girl's arms squeezed the small animal tight.

Silence.

Except for a sniffling sound out of the little girl. Eric closed his eyes for a moment. "Blessed silence."

Storey couldn't agree more.

"Can you talk to her?"

He glared at her in horror. "I don't speak Louer. No one does."

"Wrong. My stylus does."

The child rained kisses on the matted varmint. And didn't the damn thing stay like it needed the affection as much as the child did? Storey shook her head and on a corner of the first of the two papers Eric had brought, she asked her stylus if he could write Louer.

"Yes."

"Can you write a note to this child that we mean her no harm and we'd like to help her, please?"

Her hand instantly started to move, writing out weird and wonderful characters in a close, tightly woven script similar to those on the side of the stylus itself. The writing had a delicate grace to the flowing characters. When she finally stopped writing, she'd filled the top quarter of the paper. And fast. The message was illegible. "Stylus, are you sure she can't read English?"

She's too young to read written English. Her native language speaks to her differently.

"Differently how?"

But she stood up to hold the paper in front of the child. Hoping she could understand it.

The child's eyes widened as she looked at the writing, some of the fear dropped off her face and relief filled her gaze. Her gaze went from Eric, to the paper and then Storey. Tears filled her eyes and she threw herself into Storey's arms, crumpling rodent and paper together.

Storey had to wrap her arms around her. But staring at Eric over top of the girl's head, she asked, "Do you have any idea what the stylus wrote?"

"Heck no."

CHAPTER 7

THEY'D AGREED TO bring the child to Eric's home. There they could enlist Paxton's help in finding the right way to return her to her family. At the moment, they hadn't been able to do even that.

Eric couldn't get his codexes to work.

The child – they so needed to find out what her name was – had curled up in a tight ball at Storey's feet. Sleeping as if she hadn't slept in months or at least since she'd been left alone. The skorl, although not asleep if the malevolent look in its beady eyes was anything to go by, had tucked itself into the curve of the girl's waist.

Storey studied the chunky looking girl. She could see the similarities to the Louers they'd banished earlier from the Toran dimension. They were a taller, stocky race, but she hadn't had an idea of what the females looked like. She still had the broad forehead, thick nose and flat high cheekbones. Yet there was a more delicate, feminine cast to her features.

Regardless of her misgivings, the child had to be returned to her parents. That's all there was to it.

And who knew better than Storey how that process would go? "Are the codexes really broken or are you looking for a way to avoid taking us back?" Not that she'd blame him if he was. She might pull that very trick if their positions were reversed.

He snapped, "The codex problem has nothing to do with her. They worked originally, then there was a set of weird musical commands that I didn't, and still don't, understand. The last thing was a message in Toranee code that I finally understood to be your name. But before I could understand what or why, you were there, standing in front of me."

"The stylus. It probably contacted your codex to let you know my location."

Eric frowned. "Is that possible? Did he ever contact my codex before?"

It was Storey's turn to frown down at the codex. "I know it's tracked your codex, because that's how I found it when you lost it in the basement that time. But I don't know if the stylus ever tried to contact it directly. Then again, who knows."

Eric bent his head to the codex again. Once more he typed in Paxton's lab and once again, nothing happened.

"I wonder if the stylus did something so you couldn't go back without me. So I wouldn't be left here."

He glowered at her. "Then you'd better ask it."

With a soft groan, she pulled the stylus out of her pocket and grabbed the one piece of paper she had at her disposal. "Stylus, are you getting stronger?"

Yes.

She smiled triumphantly at Eric. "See. It even feels stronger in my hand."

"Yes, but is it ready to go? We need to get moving." He pointed out the sleeping pair at their feet. "We're going to have enough trouble when she wakes up. And communicating is going to be one of the biggest problems. Not to mention she'll expect us to help her and we don't even know what the stylus wrote in the message to her."

"Then let's start there with the questions." She twisted the paper so that she had a clean corner to write on. "Stylus, what did you tell the Louer girl?"

Her hand wrote quickly. *That she is safe now and that you were going to take her to her parents. And that she should trust you as you'd see her safely home.*

Eric groaned. "Why would it say that? We don't even know how to help ourselves at this point, let alone getting her home."

Storey stared at the words she'd written. "Maybe because that's how I felt." She gazed at Eric soberly. "The connection between us has deepened. It's almost as if I know what it's going to say. Maybe it has the same impression of my feelings?"

"That doesn't make sense. Why would it deepen when you'd been separated to the point where it almost went to sleep?"

"Maybe that's exactly why. To keep the connection there, to save the Louer souls inside from becoming a nothing shell like the other styluses that were outgrown, packed away and forgotten."

Storey studied the stylus in her hand. The connection did feel different. It was a little hard to explain but it felt deeper. Odd, but not unpleasant.

"Stylus, are the other styluses asleep like you were?"

Like I was in the process of becoming, yes.

"But there are souls in each one?"

Yes, especially the broken one.

She frowned. "What can we do for them?"

Nothing at the moment. Keep them safe.

"And later? Is there something we can do later?"

Yes.

Good. Glancing at Eric, she asked. "Stylus, did you do something to Eric's codex so that he couldn't leave without me?"

No. Had to change his codex to old programming to tell him you were here. His codex works but it needs to be programmed manually.

From the look of horror on Eric's face, she assumed the news wasn't to his liking.

"Stylus, can you revert the process on Eric's codex or reprogram it so we can return to Paxton's lab?"

Yes. But it takes time and energy.

Back to square one. The stylus wasn't fully up yet. Shit. The more she asked it to do, the more it wore down. And she was almost out of paper. Storey frowned. "Is there more paper here, Stylus?"

No.

"So, I have to go back to Paxton's lab to get something to write on?"

No. Go home. Paper there.

Ah. Storey sat back, an idea firing in the back of her mind.

"Why is it I don't think I'm going to like whatever you're thinking?" Eric's voice broke through her reverie.

"Let's go to my house. There's paper there, beds and food. I have no idea about my parents. We'll deal with that when we get there. Hopefully we can be there at least long enough for us to restock, reevaluate and figure out what to do. It's obvious we can't stay here. We have to go somewhere, and if you don't want to go to her new dimension, or take us to your dimension, then that only leaves my dimension." She thought she'd been the voice of reason, but from the frown on Eric's face, it didn't appear as if he agreed.

"And how are we going to get there? The codexes are on 'manual mode,' remember? Do you know how to program mine or your dimension on my codex so we can go anywhere?" he asked, the sarcasm thick on his voice.

She flipped the paper over and held up the portals. "We still have these." Although, she'd written on the portal to Bankhead mine, the other portal that she'd used to travel Paxton's lab from her bedroom, hadn't been touched. "I can change this so we can portal to my bedroom."

He closed his eyes and bowed his head. "It's not perfect, but it's better than staying in this hellhole. From there I can always go see Paxton and try to sort out the next step in this mess." With a nod toward the sleeping child, he said, "What about her?"

Storey was already working on adapting the one portal entrance. Thankfully it was almost perfect for here. She lifted her head from the sketch. "We take her with us. Believe me, I'd rather take her to her dimension right away, but not without a fully functioning stylus and lots of paper, thank you. Not to mention having your codexes working properly again." Storey shook her head. "No thank you."

"So, we hide away at your place until the stylus is stronger?" He cocked his head and waited.

"Unless you want to hide away in your dimension, instead."

"Paxton will see us. They've stepped up the monitoring of all crossings since the Louer invasion."

"Exactly."

"Fine. Let's go then. I don't know how we're going to keep her quiet though. That squeal of hers and her pet is going to cause a ruckus at your house."

"Another reason to have the stylus get back to full strength and to have more paper so he can write messages to her. If she understands we have to be quiet to get her home, then maybe – and I'm only saying maybe – she'll listen. I do know she's expecting us to solve her problems now and that includes me feeding her. Do you want to tell her there's no food when she wakes up?" She raised an eyebrow at him.

He stood. "Let's go now. I won't rest until we're out of here."

ERIC GLARED AT the codexes. How was he going to fix them?

Storey nudged his arm and pointed at the child who was starting to stir.

With an eye roll, he said, "Let's go then."

Bending over, Storey laid the paper on the floor. "I think this should work."

"Think." He didn't like the sound of that. "What if it doesn't? Can't you draw a new one?"

"Not really." She studied his expression briefly. "The stylus is not up to full power, remember? We can't overdo it."

He couldn't believe how dependent they were on technology right now. He felt naked with his codex not working properly.

"Let's go." Once again, he studied the girl and her pet. "Do we pick her up and carry her?"

"It might be best. Except for her pet. It's liable to bite your hand off."

"Yet if we wake her…"

Storey grinned at him, that clear, honest, so open grin of

hers. He couldn't help but smile back, his good humor rapidly returning. If nothing else, life with Storey was an adventure. "You're the ranger, remember. And you're the male here."

"She's no lightweight."

"So it's a good thing she isn't any older." Storey motioned toward the sleeping girl. "Now would be a good time."

Eric took a deep breath and caught up child and rodent in one scoop before either could wake. He took two steps toward Storey and walked into the portal.

STOREY WATCHED THE three disappear into her portal and whispered a prayer that this path would lead them home. She grabbed a corner of the paper and hopped in herself. The last thing she saw was the dark, dank cold of the Louer world.

Good riddance.

She tumbled into sunshine. Sunshine and nothing else – no buildings and definitely no bedroom.

"Oh shit."

"Ya think?" Eric stood beside her, still holding the sleeping child. Her pet, now awake, glared at them. Maybe as long as it was being held tight in the child's arms he wouldn't take off. Storey would have much preferred to have had it in a cage.

First things first. "Any idea where we are?"

"No. You?"

"Not yet." She turned around, puzzled. "But I will. This can only be one of three dimensions."

"Great." Eric shifted the load in his arms. "If we get caught by Louers, this isn't going to look so good."

He was right.

Time to get serious, again. "Stylus, we need help and now. I don't know where we are. We're trying to get to my house. Help."

In a shaky script, the stylus wrote, *You're only halfway. Go through the portal again.*

Storey and Eric stared at each other in horror.

Eric spun around at her words. "What. We are? Here?" He shook his head. "As in the *new* Louer dimension?"

She put the sheet of paper with the portal back on the ground. "Let's take another jump and see if it will take us to the right destination."

With a nervous glance around, Eric gave an abrupt nod and stepped in. Storey followed immediately.

And fell into her room.

"We're home," she crowed. She turned around a huge grin on her face. "Finally."

She couldn't believe how good it felt. Her bedroom. Different than she remembered, it looked like her mother had changed her bedding. Still, after all she'd been through, she was finally home. Clean clothes, a shower, food. Definitely food.

She motioned to the bed for Eric to lay the child down.

He did so carefully, asking, "What about your parents?"

Her smile fell away. "Right. That problem. Damn it." She studied Eric. How could she explain he was a ranger from another dimension and they'd brought a child of yet a third dimension and a weird pet home? What could she possibly say?

Shit. Instead of solving one problem, she had three more. Not that Eric was a problem. He was about the only good thing here.

Were her parents at home? How could she find out without drawing attention to herself and her entourage? She wanted a shower and a change of clothes so bad. The clothes she could grab. The shower – not if her parents were home. She looked out the window, realizing it was daytime. And likely early. She didn't know what day of the week or what day of the month it was, but at least the sun was shining. That meant there was a chance, a slim chance that her parents weren't home.

She opened her bedroom door and stuck her head around the corner. The house was silent. For the moment. "Eric, I'm going to slip downstairs and see if we are alone. If we are, I'll search for food. Stay here with her."

Eric frowned.

"It's the only way. Don't wake her up."

Eric's gaze widened in horror, panic starting in his eyes. "You can't leave me with her."

"I'll be back soon." She closed the door softly and crept down the hallway to her mother's room. The door was ajar and it was dark inside. Empty. That was a good sign. At the top of the stairs, she cocked an ear and listened.

So far, so good. Skipping the second stair, which squeaked, she made her way to the first landing and poked her head around the corner. Nothing. And no one. Thank heavens for that. In the den, she stopped and frowned. Different furniture. Had they bought new furniture while she'd been gone? She crossed to the corner of the den where the Louers had tried to enter the house. A smirk broke free. Typical. Her mother had already repainted.

Just to be sure, she checked the garage and front driveway and breathed a sigh of relief. There were no vehicles in sight.

She headed to the kitchen. They might have lucked out this time, but her parents could return at any time. In the kitchen she tried to find food that she could grab easily and take to her hungry guests. She collected a box of granola bars, a pound of cheese and a loaf of bread. After further hunting, she found a package of ham, a bag of apples and a bag of mini carrots. There was also a full jug of orange juice. With her large haul, she raced back up to her bedroom.

Just in time.

A rising caterwaul shrieked through the bedroom door.

"Eric. Open the door." It opened immediately, making her suspicious he'd been at the point of coming after her.

His eyes lit up at the food. She came in and dumped the food on the bed. Immediately the rodent bounced to the middle of the pile sniffing the items.

Eric raced over. "Oh no you don't." He tried to brush the animal back. The little girl, whose eyes had grown huge at the sight of the food, opened her mouth, her bottom lip trembling. "Uh, Storey. Over here, uh, like now."

Storey walked over, smiled at the girl, and opened the loaf of bread, without any butter, she slapped some ham in between two slices of bread and handed it to the child. The girl took it, her eyes huge. She looked at the sandwich and then stared up at Storey.

"I don't think she recognizes it as food."

"I'm not sure I do either, but if you make one for me, I'll be happy to demonstrate."

Storey slid him a quick look. "You don't have ham and bread in your dimension?"

"Our bread isn't white. It's dark and full of seeds and grains. And ham, no, I don't know it." She made him one and handed it over. Eric held it up to catch the little girl's attention then took a big bite and chewed. Her face lit up and she tore into her sandwich.

Storey made herself one. Looking around her bedroom, her gaze lit on the glass of water she kept beside her bed. Getting up, she dumped the contents in the sad looking plant pot. She brought the glass over and filled it with orange juice and handed it to the girl.

"We need to find a name to call her," Storey mumbled around bites.

"Tammy."

Storey looked up at him in surprise. "Is that her name?"

"Don't know. But she looks like a Tammy."

"That's fine with me, but that doesn't mean she'll answer to it."

"I think you need to show her what to do with that drink." Storey spun around to find Tammy had poked her finger into the juice.

"Oh crap." Storey lifted the glass to Tammy's mouth. Automatically, Tammy opened up and took a drink. And coughed several times. So much for being quiet.

Storey waited for a moment to make sure she was going to be fine, and held up the glass again. "Try it again."

This time Tammy drank eagerly, downing half the glass in one gulp.

"Any for me?"

She answered, "We can drink from the bottle."

Eric raised an eyebrow. He studied the bottle and lifted it to his own mouth. She watched the emotions play across his face as he tasted orange juice, and from the look on his face, maybe for the first time.

His face scrunched up, making her laugh. "It's orange juice," she said. "Made from oranges."

"Oranges?"

Oh boy. This was going to be fun. And she so didn't have time. In between bites of her sandwich, she explained. When done eating, she walked through her room and collected several changes of clothing, stuffing things into a much larger backpack she dragged out of her closet. Then she added several sketchbooks and a zip up jacket. Turning around, she perused her room taking in the familiar items of her childhood. Every time she left, she wondered if she'd ever come home again. "Is it safe to leave you three alone for a few minutes while I go wash up?"

Eric, in the middle of making a second sandwich, looked up guiltily. "Sure. We'll be fine." He slapped the second slice of bread onto the rest and Tammy snatched it out of his fingers. His look of astonishment had Storey laughing aloud.

"Good. Make yourself another one. Stay quiet, and I'll be back quick." She locked the door on her way out and headed to the bathroom. After one of the hottest, fastest, yet most satisfying showers Storey could ever remember having, she dressed in clean clothes, brushed her teeth and packed a travel bag. She didn't know when she'd be back again.

Once inside her bedroom, she paused. They were still eating. All of them.

The loaf of bread was almost gone. The meat was; the cheese almost was. Wow. She'd need to go raid the kitchen again. And soon. Yet, she couldn't help feeling that time was running out. They needed to go to Paxton's lab and get help.

She made a fast trip to the kitchen, constantly looking over her shoulder in case her parents came home. What could she take that they could eat while traveling? That she hadn't grabbed the first time, that is. The cupboard revealed grain crackers, flatbread and a package of tortillas. The second pass through the fridge harvested another package of cheese, leftover cooked chicken breasts, and more apples. Snatching up a shopping bag, she loaded it with everything. Then, going to the sideboard, she snatched up a bunch of perfectly ripe bananas. In one last pass, she collected as many of the packages of crackers as she could fit into the bag, a container of cheese spread, a spare jar of peanut butter, and a jar of jam. Snatching up several knives from the kitchen drawer, she hauled the groceries back upstairs and while the others all watched with great interest, she packed what she could in her backpack and then a second backpack for Eric to carry.

Heaving a sigh of relief she put on her sweater, and picked up another sketchbook before turning to Tammy. She realized that the little girl didn't have much to wear. Her face was badly in need of a washing and her shirt was grubby and torn. Would anything in Storey's closet fit her? Tammy was shorter but heavier, so…maybe. She rummaged in her bottom drawers for t-shirts and a pullover in case she got cold. Thank heavens it was still summer weather here.

"Eric, we need to get going. The bathroom is down the hall. I'm going to get her changed and pack a few spare items for her."

"Right. You do realize we're going to have trouble carrying all this."

Storey scanned the full bags. Was it enough? For how long? "I know. But did you see how much she ate? Do you want her running out of food and not be able to give her something? Not to mention her pet?"

He rolled his eyes. "Back in five."

Storey cleaned up the empty food packages, shaking her head at the sheer quantity of food they'd consumed. As she reached for the cheese, Tammy made a funny sound and held out her hand.

"More?" Tammy's voice thick and uncertain as the single word rolled out of her mouth. But it was understandable.

Storey grinned and broke off a decent sized piece for her. The rodent sat up on its back legs and looked at her expectantly. Storey sighed and broke off a smaller piece. She held it out and the rodent reached out to take it gently from her fingers. Maybe it was tame after all. They hadn't had a great first meeting and nothing since had endeared one to the other. But there was nothing like feeding an animal to make it a little friendlier. She wondered if Tammy had a name for it?

Standing up, she put the garbage in the can in her room, then packed the remaining food in the overstuffed bags. And went about trying to get Tammy into cleaner clothes.

Tammy didn't object, thankfully, but she made a weird mess of noises as she felt the different materials and colors. Her face lit up when Storey brought over the purple hoodie. Getting her into it and the zipper done up, was another issue altogether. Everything was so different to her; she kept playing with the zipper.

Leaving her to it, Storey spun around in her room, looking for something she'd had for her old guinea pig who'd died almost eight years ago. Stashed somewhere should be a small harness with bells and silver studs on it connected to a leash somewhere. Storey hadn't been able to get rid of it all these years. It really was time to clean up and clean out her childhood.

There. She grinned. The harness and leash hung on the back of the hanging clothes. Dragging it out, she eyed the rodent and the size of the leash when Eric walked in. His face lit up in understanding.

He grinned. "I'm so going to enjoy watching you put that on him."

"Him?"

"I don't know if it's a him or a her and I'm not checking, but you can do the honors."

Storey smirked, letting a little evil show through. "Except we really have to get going and Tammy needs to be taken to the bathroom and have her face washed. So which job do you want?"

His laugher fell away as he understood the choices. "That is so not fair." But he held out his hand in resignation.

Storey motioned for Tammy to come with her, and she led her out into the hallway, closing the door firmly behind them so Eric could do his job. In the bathroom, she spent more than a few minutes trying to show Tammy what she was supposed to do and how. Finally, giggling so hard she had tears in her eyes, Tammy got it. Storey grabbed a washcloth, warmed it up in hot water and set about scrubbing the little girl's face. By the time they were both done, the girls had laughed themselves silly. And the unmistakable odor surrounding the little girl was much improved.

Feeling better, Storey led Tammy back to the bedroom, ready to go to Paxton's place next. Opening the door to her bedroom, she found Eric sitting on the bed, the rodent happily playing with the leash, the harness buckled securely around his chest. Tammy grinned and ran over to look at the fancy chain and the colorful ribbons.

"If he's a boy, he might not appreciate the color," Storey said.

Eric looked at her, his head tilted to one side and said, "Huh?"

Storey rolled her eyes and said, "Forget it. A human joke. That's all."

He quirked one eyebrow at her. "So are we ready, or do you want to wait until your parents return?"

Even as the last of the words rolled out of his mouth, she heard the sound of a vehicle driving up the driveway. "Oh shit." Storey ran to the window to make sure, but there they were. She winced. Both of her parents were exiting the vehicle.

"Time to go. Eric, you first. And take Tammy and her pet with you."

"This is only going to take us to Stanshore Mine though, you know that. We might not be able to get out of there."

"Paxton will have the crossing monitored, and we'll be close enough to contact him." She gave him a little push, hearing her parents entering through the front door. "Go, go, go. I don't want them to find out. They'll never let me leave again."

"They won't be able to stop you as long as you have the stylus," he reminded her.

"Yeah, thanks for that." She was already scribbling a note on a piece of school paper. "What are you waiting for? Get moving," she whispered. Eric shouldered the largest backpack and held out his hand for Tammy. Storey picked up the rodent and as one they stepped into the portal.

In a flash they were gone. "Thank goodness for that." She took a quick look around. It was obvious someone had been in her room, there was no way to help that. Storey dropped the note on her bed. Hearing footsteps coming up the stairs, she grabbed the other backpack, and hanging onto a corner of her portal picture, she entered, dragging the paper through with her. She didn't dare leave it behind for her parents to accidentally fall through.

The last thing she heard, was her mother's hopeful voice calling her, "Storey, honey, is that you?"

And the sound of the door opening followed by her mother's gasp of surprise.

Then all Storey could see was blackness.

They'd gotten out just in time. As much as relief pulsed through her, so too did a pang of homesickness. Her mother didn't deserve this. Surely she could have stayed behind long enough to reassure her that everything was okay. But she wouldn't have understood and Storey couldn't explain, not now, and not in any way that would do any good.

Maybe that note would help ease her mother's pain.

Or maybe not.

CHAPTER 8

STOREY LANDED OFF center and fell forward onto her knees. "Shit."

Eric stepped forward and grabbed her elbow. "Are you okay?"

It took her a moment, but then she stood up unsteadily, more from the panic of leaving and the remorse of hurting her family than her fall. "I'm fine. My mother walked in as I left."

"She didn't see you, did she?"

"No. I just heard her call and the door open as I went through." Storey sighed, already wishing she'd stayed and said something. "Maybe I should have stayed and explained things to her."

"Do you really think you could have?"

"No." And she didn't. Still, the warm concern in Eric's voice made her straighten and smile reassuringly at him. Fatigue lined his face. He hadn't had it easy either, this last week. Unlike her, he hadn't had a shower.

And somehow, Tammy had gone from standing beside him to riding piggyback. Eric didn't appear to mind, even when the rodent sat up on his shoulder to stare down at Storey.

She had to grin. Eric had gained two friends. Turning around, she scanned the familiar mine. "Any idea if your codex will work here?"

"It should. It's a number code only for there. If you're ready, let's go before Paxton wonders what we're doing here." He started punching in numbers. The resulting musical ringtones made her chuckle. How many times had she heard those? They almost sounded like a homecoming party. Seeing the start of the black fog rising around their ankles, she stepped closer. "Hope this works."

Through the deafening stillness, he said, "Me too."

She shuddered at the thought of anything else going wrong. Honest to God, she needed something to go right for a change.

"We're here." Eric's warm, comforting voice had her opening her eyes to see his staring into hers, amusement lighting their dark depths. Her response was instant. A warm smile unfurled. "Sorry, I'm still not used to that." Tammy's huge saucer eyes staring at her, her arms wrapped in a vice grip around Eric's neck.

"Easy, Tammy. It's all right." Storey reached a soothing hand to stroke Tammy's knee, feeling some of the rigidity leave her stocky frame.

He stretched his neck slightly, easing the tightness. "Is she okay? She's getting heavy."

"Harrumph."

Eric and Storey stilled and turned as one to stare at Paxton. Storey grinned and threw herself into his arms. "Paxton!"

He flushed multiple shades of white and pink, his arms closing awkwardly around her. "Storey, what happened to you?"

She pulled back, her smile flashing even brighter at his obvious embarrassment. She couldn't help looking around, delighted to see the familiar lab. Everything pristine white, all surfaces bare and clean, monster-sized monitors filling the room so he and his assistants could track all activity regarding dimension crossings.

"It's so great to be back here. I know I wasn't gone for long, but it seemed like forever."

"But where were you?"

"In the Louer dimension. Compliments of your leader, I believe," she added darkly.

His eyes widened in horror. "Oh dear. I'd so hoped he wasn't involved." Paxton lifted his head to look at Eric, his face pale, his eyes disturbed. "Eric?"

Storey was looking at Paxton when it happened. He bolted backwards, his eyes widening in horror. His jaw worked but no sound came out.

"Oh no. Here it comes." Eric tried to shift Tammy off his back so he could explain her presence to Paxton. Immediately the horrific wailing erupted from her mouth.

"Oh God, Eric, we have to make her stop." Storey raced over. "Tammy, stop. It's all right. Please stop."

Tammy buried her face against Eric's back and screamed at the top of her lungs. Storey reached into her backpack for the cheese she'd put in at the end. Ripping off a chunk, she held the piece out to Tammy. "Here, Tammy, cheese."

Tammy's head tilted her way, her nose wrinkled in spite of the piercing noise still coming out of her mouth. Her eyes opened and her gaze latched on to the cheese. Instantly the noise stopped as she started eating the treat with tiny bites.

Eric's shoulders slumped with relief. "I don't know what you gave her, but please tell me you have enough to keep her happy until she's returned to her parents."

Storey laughed. "Yeah, that I can't do. I'm hoping she'll

take other food too, though." She held out her arms to Tammy and with a gamin grin, Tammy dropped like a stone from Eric's back and ran to Storey, wrapping her arms around her middle.

Groaning, Eric straightened. "She is not a lightweight."

"What…what is she?" Paxton cleared his throat several times, his gaze locked on Tammy's face. He shook his head. "No, she can't be."

Eric walked over to his old mentor. "Paxton, it's okay. She's only a child." He quickly explained, ending with, "She was the only Louer left in her complex. We couldn't leave her there."

Paxton's head had swiveled from Eric's face to Tammy's and back again several times. There was no softening in his features at the explanation, but Storey could see his mind spin with the options. "We couldn't leave her behind, Paxton. She had no food, no clothing, no one."

With another quick shift to look at Storey, Paxton asked, "Why didn't they go back and get her?"

Eric looked over at Storey. "According to Storey's stylus, there's something wrong with the portal. They can't return to their old world. Effectively cutting off both groups from each other. The complex where we found her is empty. I doubt she knows about any other complexes given her age. I'm sure she'd have died if we'd left her."

At Eric's last words, some of the rigidity in Paxton's spine and his shoulders relaxed slightly. Thank heavens for that. Paxton wasn't the boss here, but he held a lot of power.

"Thank you for understanding." Storey did appreciate it. As she'd already found out, having Paxton on her side was huge.

Paxton said, "You're going to take her home?" It wasn't

a question as much as statement of fact.

"Well—"

But Storey cut Eric off in midsentence. "Yes. I'm going to take her back to her family."

Paxton nodded once as if he'd expected no less. "What do you need?"

Storey explained, "My stylus went into some kind of power saver mode while we were separated over in the Louer dimension, but it's taking a long time to recharge. I want to make sure it's fully functioning before traveling again. Also, because it was having trouble communicating, the stylus switched the codex to using Toranee code, or something." Storey turned to Eric. "Right?"

"The stylus can't reverse the change until it's back to full power."

"We'll need to reset the function panel." Paxton latched onto the one thing he could do something about. "Give it to me." Eric took off both machines and handed them over. Paxton bent his head, muttering to himself. "Yes. Interesting. Haven't seen this in decades. Hmmm." He walked over to one of the desks and pulled out a series of wires and odd black rubber attachments.

"Ah Eric, I think we need to tell Paxton about the rodent, too. Before he finds out the hard way."

Eric rolled his eyes. "Smart." He walked over to where Paxton worked. "Paxton, we forgot to mention that Tammy has her pet with her. That's the reason she missed the move to the other dimension, so we figured we'd better bring it too."

"Pet? What pet?" His gaze turned from Eric to Storey before latching onto Tammy's face. The rodent sat on Tammy's shoulder, his cheerful harness and leash looking bizarre against his dark fur. "Oh dear. Yes. Yes, please keep it on that leash at all times. Oh dear." He shook his head once and turned back to the table and the codexes in front of him.

Eric walked back to Storey. "See? Easy."

"We'll see about that. So far, nothing has been easy," he retorted, his wry grin belying the sharpness of his words. "How do we find out what the stylus needs to return to full health?"

Storey didn't need to think about that. "We ask it. But the more we ask of it right now, the less it can rejuvenate."

"What then?" Eric raised an eyebrow in question.

"Then we ask Paxton's stylus what it needs."

Eric sat back, a frown on his face. "Oh. That makes sense."

"Can we sit somewhere? I'd like to grab a sketchbook and see how the stylus is doing."

Eric pointed to the table where she'd sat toward the end of the celebration they'd had the night before. She stopped. Night before? Surely it had been longer. And it might have been. Time had become beyond screwy.

Leading Tammy over, she pulled out chairs for both of them and showed Tammy how to use one. Tammy grinned and bounced on the chair several times. Only stilling her antics long enough to watch curiously as Storey opened her bag to remove a sketchbook. Tammy grabbed it and tried to bite the end.

"No. This isn't food." Storey dove back into her bag and pulled out a red apple. She handed it to Tammy who looked at it and frowned. Storey took a bite, showed Tammy the inside. Tammy immediately bit into the apple. Her eyes grew rounder and she bounced several more times.

"I think she likes it," murmured Eric.

"Good thing. We know what happens when there's something she doesn't like." She hurriedly looked away as the skorl took a bite from the other side of Tammy's apple. Shudders rippled across her back. She so didn't want to share her meal with that thing.

Opening her sketchbook, she pulled out her stylus and studied the markings on the side. Now if only she knew what they meant. Something she'd have to ask her stylus about later.

"Stylus, we need information." She held her hand over the corner of a blank page of her sketchbook. "What do you need to get to full power?"

Time.

"Why is it taking so long?"

Damaged.

"Damaged?" Eric and Storey both bent to study the pencil. Twisting and turning it, neither could see any damage. "What kind of damage?"

Souls. We are getting older. Will need a new soul soon.

"Soon? As in how soon?" Storey frowned at Eric.

Within the next decade.

Storey and Eric both relaxed. "Good. That gives us a little time to figure that part out. Somehow. So it takes longer for you to recharge once we've been separated. Do the other styluses need new souls too?

Yes.

"Are the ones in there still alive?" Storey couldn't imagine their existence.

We are always in stasis. New souls will blend and all will be well.

Eric looked at Storey and shook his head. "I don't think so."

Storey studied his features. "Don't think what?"

"It's not all going to be well. We don't know how to blend souls into the stylus anymore, and even if we did, it would be against our laws to force someone to do so."

"What about volunteers? Chances are someone would be interested in living forever."

He scrunched his face in disgust. "Not me."

Storey frowned. "If my life was almost over, it would be a heck of a way to extend it. To help out my people."

"Go for it. You're not locking me inside a pencil forever."

Storey had to laugh at the way he said it. It might not be right for him, but if her people were involved she could see a long line forming almost instantly. Especially those with a terminal illness. To live forever was a much sought after goal with her people. The novelty alone would peak interest around the globe. She could see riots happening as people vied for the dozen odd positions.

Eric glanced over at Paxton working away on his codex. "It's not an issue right now, anyway. We need to find the correct codes to take Tammy home. Can the stylus help us do that?"

"Probably."

The longer Tammy was with her, the less she looked like a Louer and the more she resembled a normal child. Speaking of which…

"I haven't seen many children in your dimension?" Eric's face twisted curiously. "Don't you guys believe in families?" she said.

The faintest pink color washed over his face. "We do, but not large ones and many people are choosing to have no children."

She didn't know what more to say to that. Paxton worked at his desk on the codexes How much had he heard? He'd stayed out of it so far, but they knew so much more about her world and she knew so little about theirs. "Sounds like both of our systems need overhauling. Not that I know much about your world."

Paxton came over, the codexes in his hand. "And that might be for the best. If you are ever captured by your government and tortured for information, you won't have any to give them."

Stilling, Storey sucked her cheeks in. Was Paxton kidding? Not that she'd ever heard him do so before. Still the thought of her government trying to get information out of her made her skin crawl.

Her feelings must have shown on her face because Eric reached out and placed a comforting hand on her shoulder. "That's not going to happen." He smiled reassuringly at her.

But what did he know?

A small hand crept under hers. Tammy. Storey put on a happy face for her. Keeping her voice light and soothing, she said, "It's okay. Everything will be fine."

"Hmpph. Says you," Paxton grumped, "You need to take her home before anyone else finds out she's here."

"I'd like to. The longer she's away, the harder it is on her, too." Storey pulled off her sweater and set it on the chair. She picked up the codexes. "So Eric will be able to use these now? Easily?"

Paxton went to speak then stopped. Storey stared at him but he silently pointed at the marks on her arm. She shrugged. "I don't know how, where, or when I got them."

Luckily Paxton stayed quiet, thinking heavily if his furrowed brow and distant gaze was anything to go by. Storey exchanged looks with Eric. He raised one brow but stayed quiet.

After a moment, Paxton continued as if the subject of her new honor marks had never been brought up. "Yes. I've recalibrated their functions. Everything is normal."

"Perfect." She watched as Eric picked up the closest codex, his fingers checking the systems until he was satisfied they were working properly. "Are you good now?"

"Yes." He clipped the first one on his wrist. Pushing the second one her way, he added, "Put that one on."

As instructed, she clipped hers on. Tammy made ooing sounds at the shiny look of it. Together the two girls admired the flashy armband. Tammy held out her arm. Paxton shook his head hard enough for his hair to fly off in all directions again.

Tammy's face puckered up.

Eric's voice cut through the room. "Storey, look out."

Just in time, Storey pulled a granola bar from her pocket. The shiny, brightly colored wrapper instantly caught Tammy's attention. Her eyes lit up and she grabbed it from Storey's hand. Turning it over and around, she admired all the colors.

"I don't think she knows she can eat it."

"You mean eat what's in it. We don't want her eating the wrap—"

Tammy shoved one end of the bar, wrapper and all in her mouth and bit down.

"Oh shit." Storey tried to take the bar away from her, but Tammy's eyes widened and her teeth clamped down even harder.

Storey dug into her bag and dragged out a second bar. Sitting back in front of Tammy again, she ripped open one end and took the flat bars out. Tammy blinked, watching Storey's every move. Then Storey took a bite of one of the two bars, and put the bright wrapper on the table.

In the sudden silence she realized several things. The first was that Tammy appeared to understand the concept of wrappers as she removed the packaged bar from her mouth and worked at ripping the end off like she'd seen Storey do; and two, the two men were staring at the spare half of the granola bar in her hand.

Her gaze widened as Eric swallowed. With a big sigh, and realizing that males appeared to be the same whether in her dimension or Eric's, she held out the unbitten piece to Paxton and the half with the bite taken out of it to Eric.

Both men accepted and bit into the treat; Eric, with obvious relish, and Paxton, with great interest but also trepidation. Eric had already eaten food at her house, whereas Paxton had very little experience with anything human – just her.

"It's okay Paxton. It might be different to you but it's perfectly edible."

He raised his gaze to her as he bit hard and the honey and almond flavor filled his mouth. He reared back slightly and blinked. "What is it?"

"We call it a granola bar. It's food that we use for traveling, snacks and even kids' lunches."

Eric hadn't wasted time on words, having finished his half in a few bites. "If you don't like it, that's fine. I'll eat it."

Paxton frowned at him. "It's good."

A small hand came to rest on Storey's shoulder. She turned to face Tammy to see her holding out the second half of her granola bar for Storey to share.

Storey's heart melted a little more. "Thank you, Tammy." As much as she didn't care to eat the granola bar, Tammy was clearly expecting her to have some. Deviating from that was likely to upset her. Storey reached out to accept it. She took a small bite then offered it back to her. Tammy's eyes lit up and her face beamed. She took the bar back and finished it in several bites.

"Whew. Good thing you packed a mess of food. That girl can eat." Eric's voice was an awed whisper that reminded Storey of the boys in her school back home. The more time she spent with Eric and Tammy, the more she realized that, regardless of their dimension, people were all essentially the same.

And saying that aloud wouldn't make her popular at all.

Storey considered just how much she'd changed over this last week. No longer was her mother an oddity, or her ex-boyfriend a devastating loss. High school was no longer something to get through, but an opportunity to learn. She wondered if her school taught classes in outdoor living, astronomy, or navigation. All things she'd love to explore. Doubtful they'd have courses in alternative dimensions, travel by codex or Toran and Louer history.

She grinned at the thought. They'd be awesome classes though. Although the only human in a position to teach would be her – and her education in these areas was sadly lacking.

Maybe she could persuade Eric to come back and teach her people. *Not likely.*

"What are you snickering about?"

Storey dropped her smile. "Sorry. I was just thinking how hard it's going to be to go back to school. The courses I want to take won't be offered."

"It does make one consider how different reality can be."

Eric nodded to Tammy.

Storey understood. "And like my stylus. That's so far beyond anything I'd have been able to imagine."

"Yet dimensions were totally believable."

Holding up the splayed fingers of her right hand, she counted off all the movies she'd seen with different realities and dimensions, "Star Trek, Inception, Harry Potter, Army of Darkness, Dinotopia." At the blank look on everyone's faces, she laughed. "They're all movies I've watched about different dimensions. We've been exploring the idea of you guys for decades. We have books and shows dedicated to such concepts."

"And how does reality match up?" Eric's eyes lit with humor.

Paxton stepped in. "I would like to know what shows and movies are?"

Storey opened her mouth to explain when the door opened to the lab and someone she'd met on her last trip raced inside. Memories flashed through Storey's mind of the cute young Toran fighting in the war against the Louers. She stood and grinned at him. "Hi, Jendron."

He came to a complete stop and stared at her in surprise. His face lit up. "Hi. You're back already?"

"I didn't get a chance to go home yet."

Confusion clouded Jendron's face as he tried to work that out.

Paxton didn't give him a chance. "Jendron. Why have you come?"

His face cleared. "The Councilman hasn't shown up for the meeting. The other council members haven't been able to locate him. I've been sent to ask you for your help."

Eric stood up. "Paxton, is my father still missing?"

Paxton frowned, walking over to the control center. "Apparently."

Storey worked hard to keep her mouth shut. Inside she wanted to jump up and down for joy. Maybe the Councilman would stay missing. Lord knows, the Torans would be better off. Then she remembered that although nasty and mean, he was still Eric's father.

Paxton started working a series of keys. She wanted to go over and see what he was doing, but she suddenly became aware of Jendron's horrified stare.

"Eric."

Eric turned from Paxton's side to look at her, a question on his face. She nodded toward Jendron. Eric glanced over, then followed the direction of Jendron's gaze.

He sighed. "Jendron. Report to the Council that we are searching for the Councilman. As we are currently involved in a separate issue of the State, it is imperative that you speak of nothing you have seen here. That includes Storey's return at this time."

Jendron tore his gaze away from Tammy and her pet. His mouth opened as if to speak but Paxton glowered at him, effectively silencing any comments.

In a quiet voice, but one that brooked no arguments, Paxton said, "If you are unable to follow these orders, you will state so now, and work in another part of the government will be found for you. Do you understand?"

The huge Adams' apple in his long throat bobbed repeatedly. Finally, Jendron nodded. "Yes. I understand. My apologies."

He backed out of the room. As he went to close the door again, Storey called out, "Thanks, Jendron. It's good to see you again."

His grin flashed her way before the door shut.

ERIC WALKED OVER. "You shouldn't encourage him. He won't understand."

Storey looked at him in apparent surprise. "Is letting him know that I'm happy to see him encouraging him? I was just being friendly."

The clacking of keys came to a dead stop. Paxton turned in surprise. "What are you discussing?"

"Eric was just warning me not to be too friendly to Jendron." Her cheeky grin widened at Paxton's expression. "Guess you really wouldn't like that either, huh? No permanent residence here for me."

Weird noises came from Paxton as he continued to stare at her in dawning dismay.

Eric frowned. "Paxton are you all right?"

But Paxton's eyes were wide with shock. "It can never be. You know that, right?"

Walking closer, Eric reached out to his old friend. "It's okay, Paxton. Jendron knows the score. I just don't want anyone to get the wrong impression of Storey. She's unique. Brilliant actually. Of course the males are going to be interested."

He shot Storey a warning look as her snicker reached him. It was Paxton he was worried about. Obviously the fact that Storey was an attractive, dynamic female hadn't occurred to him or the potential problems that could arise. Eric didn't know what role he wanted her to play in his life; he just knew that he wanted her there. Only time would tell how strong the feelings were.

Life with Storey could never be boring. The relationships he'd seen between Toran mates were so peaceful and quiet that he didn't understand what kept them going. Did people talk together? Did they do anything outside of meal times? He didn't know. Paxton lived alone. His father lived alone. His peers were all like him. Young and single. The few married couples he'd met were on Council.

The decline in formal marriages might have had some effect on the declining population. He couldn't imagine being a father. Yet, he'd watched Storey with Tammy and she'd been a natural mother. He didn't think of any of the women he'd gone out with that could have handled the situation as easily.

Storey had definitely made him rethink what he wanted in a mate. And everyone looked drab and pale beside her color and energy.

"Eric?"

Shaking his head, Eric turned back to Paxton. "I'm here."

Paxton's gaze locked him in place. "Make sure you're here one hundred percent. Don't split your energies...or your loyalties."

Was that a warning? If so, of what? And why?

Chapter 9

"WE NEED TO get Tammy home," Storey said. "And soon."

"That's what I'm trying to make happen here." Paxton snapped. "We need to find the Councilman and you need to return that…that thing to her new home."

"That thing has a name – Tammy." Storey pointed out Tammy to the men. The little girl had curled up asleep on the floor. She never asked for anything and appeared to be comfortable without any creature comforts. Then, when she remembered the lack of luxuries in the Louer dimension, Tammy probably wasn't used to much more. "At least that's the name we've been calling her." And that was pretty arrogant of them. Pulling out her stylus, she asked, "Stylus, do you know the name of the Louer child we have with us?"

Louers' names are based on their parents' names.

She shrugged. "Does that mean you don't know then?"

I would need to know her parents' names.

"Are you feeling better, Stylus?" Storey got up to check the sleeping child for markings. Nothing visible. Walking back to the table and her paper, she said, "Tammy doesn't appear to have any marks on her."

Tammy? If you have her name why do you ask me for it? Yes, I am feeling better.

Storey chuckled. "Because it's not her real name, it's just

a name we made up." She turned toward Eric. "The stylus says he's feeling better."

"Good. Can we go then?"

"Stylus, are you now strong enough to locate this child's family so we can return her to them?"

Yes.

"Woot! Okay. How do we take her home?"

I can give you the location of where their portal landed.

"All of which is good news." Storey started to collect the few items she'd pulled from her bag in preparation for the upcoming journey.

"Can you give us the coordinates for Eric to program into the codexes?"

Yes. The stylus rattled off a series of numbers.

"Stylus, is there something I should know about trying to return Tammy to the Louers?"

A humming sound filled the air again. Just the sound perked her up. The stylus could make sounds but not speak. Knowing how and why would make her life easier. Then again, so would so many other things.

Her hand jerked so she put the stylus to paper and watched the words form. *They will not appreciate what you've done. Neither will they thank you.*

Great, so not fun. "Is there a way to deliver Tammy without upsetting them?"

No.

"Would they accept it easier if I went alone?

No. Once they understand that it was you and Eric who sent the other Louers back during the skirmish then they will capture you and keep you imprisoned.

"And their punishment would be what?" She didn't really want to hear this, but figured it was better to know what they were dealing with. Maybe it wasn't so bad.

Death.

She rolled her eyes. Of course. Eric placed a warm hand on her shoulder. "Sounds almost familiar, doesn't it?"

"Sure does." For all the seriousness of the mission and potential outcome, she appreciated Eric's grounded humor. "I *can* go alone. There's no point in both of us getting caught."

"And that's enough of that. I should have taken you home last time. There's no way I'm letting you go blindly into something like this. We need to deliver her and get out. Fast."

"Sounds good to me." She stood and gazed into his eyes. "What's the chance of that happening?"

He frowned. "Not much, but we're not without resources. They won't understand what we're doing or that we're only trying to help, so there's no point in trying to make them."

Eric's words sounded good, but like her, he knew how much could go wrong. "Let's get started then."

FOR ALL THEIR good intentions, it wasn't a fast process. Eric needed to do a couple of trial runs with the codexes. Paxton couldn't find the coordinates given by the stylus and Storey needed to give Tammy more food. She'd tried to explain that they were taking her home to her family but Tammy just stared blankly.

Eric spoke up. "Why don't you get the stylus to write a note to her again?" He stood, hands on his hips watching as the stylus wrote a message in a language his own people didn't know. Paxton, once he understood what was happening, raced over to try and read the message himself.

He glanced at Eric, a question on his face.

"No, I don't understand it either." Eric explained, "It's the same language that's written on the side of the styluses."

Paxton pulled his stylus out of his pocket to study the faded markings on his. "I'd never noticed."

"According to Storey, it has meaning as to the souls inside."

"Like the names of those soulbound?" He frowned and walked back to his desk. From the look on his face he was planning on researching any connection to his stylus he could find.

Eric finally turned back to Storey. Her bag was packed and Tammy bounced beside her, obviously happy with the message the stylus had given her.

"Is there any reason why the stylus can't write a message to the Louers and explain what we're doing and why?"

The look of surprise on her face irritated him. "I do get some good ideas, too, you know."

She flushed. "Sorry. It's a great idea." She dropped her backpack and pulled out her sketchbook. "Stylus, can you write a note for us to give to the Louers to explain why we have Tammy with us and that we are only trying to get her home. Would that work?"

It might.

"Good. We'd want her to have such a note anyway, as an explanation of how she'd arrived there."

The stylus scripted out a long message on the paper. After it was done, Storey carefully stored it in the outside pocket of her backpack for easy access.

"Okay, let's go." She picked up the bag and grabbed Tammy's hand. "We're ready."

Now if only Eric was. He couldn't help thinking this mission was a bad idea. Only there was no doubt that Tammy needed to go home. Damn. What happened to his old, boring life? Now look at him. Saving a child. Helping a damsel to fulfill her quest. This was the stuff of heroes.

And he was going to be the hero.

"Eric? You can change your mind."

He grinned. "No way. I'm not going to miss out on any adventure available to me." *I don't want to go back to life like it used to be. It will happen soon enough. I'll take all the memories and store them away for the long future ahead of me.*

She looked up at him, admiration and pride washing over her pretty face.

Warmth spread through him. It felt right.

"Paxton, old friend, we're leaving. Please keep the lines open and your stylus on you at all times. This could be the worst mission ever."

Paxton's wrinkled face twisted with worry. "Are you sure you should be doing this?"

"No, but it's got to be done. Tammy needs her family and we need her away from here."

Eric held out a hand for Storey.

She placed hers in his. Trust. His back straightened. He grinned at her. "Ready?"

STOREY TOOK A deep breath as she waited for the black mist to rise up around her. Doing the right thing didn't always feel good. There was no doubt what they were doing was right for Tammy, but for herself and Eric, well…

A small hand crept into hers.

Another piece of Storey's heart melted. She looked at

Tammy as she squeezed in between Eric and herself. Skorky, the name Storey had given the pet, sat comfortably on Tammy's shoulder. For all her inability to communicate, Tammy got her message across just fine. Outside of her couple attempts at speech, she'd stayed quiet – except for the horrific sounds that came out of her mouth when she was upset.

Squeezing the small hand, Storey found herself wishing she could hold Eric's hand. As soon as she'd dismissed the concept, Eric wrapped both arms around the girls. Tammy grinned and laid her head against Storey's chest. There was no sign of Skorky now. Oh there, it had slipped into Tammy's hood, its leash secure in Tammy's hand. Storey shuddered. She so didn't want that thing near her, but it would be worse if it escaped again. Paxton would have a fit.

Not to mention Tammy's reaction.

The blackness rose higher, making Storey's stomach heave. She'd been getting better at portal travel but this trip was unnerving to begin with. Still she'd made as many preparations as she could. Knowing they could end up in the middle of a group of angry Louers and have everything stolen again, she'd fashioned a chain with an odd piece of material that was similar to string, only more plasticized. With the stylus safely secured, she'd hung it around her neck to rest close to her heart. Just to be sure, she'd also folded several pieces of paper, stuffing them into her different pockets and hiding places.

The last thing she wanted was to lose her one advantage to getting home. The other styluses were safe with Paxton. He'd held them with such reverence; she knew they'd be safe with him.

The codexes had been preprogrammed to come to Paxton's lab. As long as she remembered to enter the numbers in the correct sequence. Eric had explained all that, but she'd only paid attention when he added it was a safety precaution in case they became separated.

Getting separated was *not* in her plans, but should anything happen…

Eric's fingers squeezed her shoulder. Storey realized her eyes had closed and she'd tucked her head against his shoulder. She hated that nerves were eating her alive this time.

"It'll be okay, Storey. We can do this."

Her spirits lifted. When his gaze caught hers, she grinned. "You're right. We can. I just wish we already had."

The mist dropped away.

Her breath gushed out.

They were in a meadow. Brilliant clear skies shone above them. Warm fresh air filled her senses. Spectacular. No smog. No pollution. No Louers.

She turned in a circle as a thought hit her. "Do you build houses with your hands?"

Out of the blue and totally unrelated to anything – yeah, real smooth Storey. She sighed at the strange look on his face and explained, "I thought I'd created a copy of my world but maybe I created a copy of the original – without human interference. Although, given the vegetation, they must have an ecosystem of some kind. Hopefully that included wildlife."

"Really. We're here in the new Louer dimension, potentially facing grave danger and you want to know if I can build a house with my hands."

His astonishment had her laughing. She spread her arms wide. "Look around. There's no sign of civilization. For some reason I thought there'd be a city here but why would there be? They haven't had time to build anything. For all I know, these people are hiding in caves or tents."

His strange look got even stranger and then his shoulders started to shake. Finally loud guffaws erupted, his beautiful voice rolling over the hills. Not the smartest thing, considering the circumstances. Herding Tammy toward a large group of fir trees at the edge of the meadow, she demanded, "Just what is so funny? Geesh. You guys travel through dimensions like you're taking a Sunday stroll. Is it so strange to see that I might wonder if you can throw together cities in a day or two?"

He tried to answer, but his chuckles prevented it. He did, however, follow them to the relatively hidden position behind the trees.

Storey peered through the trees in all directions. Satisfied that no one waited to pounce on them, she turned back to Eric who still had a big grin on his face.

"So. How quickly would the Louers have created shelters for themselves?"

His laughter stopped to be replaced with surprise as if he finally understood the basis for her earlier query. "I don't know. But that's a good question."

She sighed. "Do you think they could have something pulled together by now? I'm just trying to get an understanding of what they might be doing at this point."

"I would suspect they've hidden away somewhere to assess their new location. The landscape is so different from their old home, they have to be concerned. Probably sent out a party to look around, and left the others behind. Alternatively, if they have some technology, they could have thrown up a temporary center already."

"Not helpful. Let's go." Storey lifted her backpack then held her hand to Tammy. The two started walking forward.

"Hey, where are you going?" Eric followed along. "Do you know where they are?"

"Nope. But I hear water. That's where I'd set up camp first."

"Oh." They walked in silence until the sound of rushing water was loud enough to really hear. Tammy tried to pull her hand free and run closer, but Storey wasn't sure she knew how to swim. There'd been no evidence of water in her dimension at all. Although there had to have been as Tammy would still need fluids.

"Hold on Tammy." But Tammy wasn't happy with that. She pulled and tugged harder. Rather than taking the chance of her starting to scream and bring a pack of angry Louers down on her, Storey increased the pace until she was almost running.

They crashed through small bushes to arrive at the edge of a small river. A small waterfall was the cause of the noise. Up above, where the water poured over the rocks, she could see the river widened into a wide, lazy stream. They could probably cross it on foot. Tammy was fascinated. She ran her fingers in the water and tried to splash around. Storey hung on to her with one hand and in the other hand she held the leash for the rodent. He'd survived the misty crossing and now wanted to explore. The two of them could do all the exploring they wanted – as soon as they were someone else's responsibility.

Handing the leash to Eric, Storey bent and scooped up water in her one hand and took a drink. Eric gave a shocked gasp. The second sip tasted even better. Raised in a small town like she had been, she'd often drunk from rivers and streams. Most city people wouldn't. That was their problem.

"What?"

"Is that safe to drink?" He almost shouted. "Just like that. You don't test it or anything?"

"Yes, just like that. I created this dimension to be a replica of my dimension. The water on my side is safe to drink, at least in many parts of the world, and without people to mess it up, it should be lovely and fresh. And it is." She lifted her hand toward him. "Try it."

He looked doubtful, but Tammy needed no urging, she went down on her hands and knees and put her face in the water like a dog and drank. Then she dunked her face all the way in and came up laughing. She shook her head, sending water droplets flying in all directions.

Storey and Eric laughed at her antics.

"There is so much I wish I could ask her. Like if she had water like this in her old home? Did they have trees and sky there? We saw so little and what we saw wasn't the most welcoming."

"I know. Do her people know what's edible over here? Do they know how to grow their food? Their population is so small, do they know how to survive here?"

"There is so much we don't know. They made a mass exodus from their dimension, but did they come with food, animals, tools, or hunting skills even, so can they survive here? Or have we just changed the type of prison they live in?"

"Stop feeling guilty. You've done a lot for them. They'll have to learn to help themselves, too."

"I know. I just can't help but wonder how they are doing. To have found Tammy as we did, well, I just can't imagine her being left there all alone like that."

"Well, she isn't any longer. We've brought her this far. We'll get her home."

He turned to look around.

"Uh, Storey."

"Hmmm." She was busy scooping handfuls of fresh water and drinking from her hand. Most of the water ran away before she could. But she didn't dare release Tammy's hand so she could scoop with two hands. Tammy was liable to walk out into the middle of the water. Tammy was well on her way to being soaked just from the shore.

"Storey?" Eric shook her shoulder. Gently at first. Then roughly. "Storey!"

"What?" she said in exasperation. Only his silence and odd stance caught her attention.

His tone of voice was hushed and wary. "Company."

Oh shit.

From her crouched position, Storey studied Tammy's face. Only the girl didn't appear to have noticed the new arrivals. What did that mean? She tugged on Tammy's hand, hoping to get her attention too. As Storey straightened, Tammy was automatically tugged upwards, too.

Tammy's face puckered. She turned to face Storey, a cry about to come forth when she froze.

"Oh shit."

"More like double shit."

CHAPTER 10

STOREY TURNED EVER so slowly. She gasped. A quick scan of Tammy's face showed no joy either. Her bottom lip trembled. Not good. Her hand clenched Storey's and she snuggled tight against her side. Definitely not good. Were the strangers even Tammy's people?

The two people walking cautiously toward them were female and definitely made Tammy appear more childlike in comparison. Chunky, stocky, thick featured, they were similar to the males that Storey remembered shipping home to their dimension.

Did they know who Storey and Eric were?

They'd taken in Tammy's presence but their features in no way showed that they recognized her as one of their own people.

"Eric?" She kept her voice calm and quiet.

He answered in an equally low murmur, "Yeah. I'm here. Not sure what to do at this point."

Not liking the situation, she stepped closer to him. Tammy stayed glued to her side. "Tammy isn't liking this development."

"That's not good." He bent around her slightly to see for himself.

She waited, considering their options. The Louers were still a bit away. "Do we run?"

"Where?" he countered.

Damn. "Suggestions?"

"None."

"Aren't you the ranger here? Don't you speak multiple languages? Can't you communicate with them at least?" With a sharp motion, she tapped his codex. "Why are your codexes not translators, too?"

He lifted his arm. "That capability has never been needed before. I would have to ask Paxton about adding such a function."

"Right." The two were almost upon them. Storey stiffened at the stony looks on their faces. She tried smiling at them. No reaction. "Being friendly isn't helping."

"Pull out the message from your stylus."

"Oh right." Awkwardly, trying to keep an eye on the approaching women while working to open the pocket on her backpack, Storey finally managed to pull out the note. She straightened. Eric took it from her, unfolded it, then held it up in front of them.

The women stopped. Something flashed in their eyes. When they were still a good fifteen feet away, Storey called out, "Hello. It's nice to see you."

Both women had similar features, potentially making them siblings. Except one had short, dark hair and the hair on the other one was a lighter brown. The dark haired one glared at her.

"Great. Tammy doesn't speak verbally either. What's the chance they can communicate telepathically and sounds bother them?" she whispered.

"Noise didn't appear to bother Tammy. But telepathic communication might explain Tammy's lack of speech."

The women separated several feet as they approached.

One came up on the outside of Eric and the other on the outside of Storey. Tammy freaked. Her mouth opened and the shrillest sound they'd heard yet came out of her mouth. Storey gasped and clapped her hands over her ears. From under her half closed lids, she could see the two women still strode forward. The noise didn't affect them.

"Maybe they're deaf."

"That would be wonderful right now."

Shuddering against the shrill tones, Storey bent to wrap her arms around Tammy. The shrieks reduced to whimpers. And Tammy locked her arms around Storey's neck – tight.

For a child, she was strong. Then she was going to grow into one of those Amazon women. Still, lifting her was out of the question. After a few moments, Tammy calmed enough to lift her face away from Storey's shirt.

Something poked her side. Storey turned to see one of the women had a long pole in her hand, and where that had come from she didn't know. Eric was receiving similar attention.

She frowned at the women and whispered, "What do they want?"

"To see how fat we are. To see if we're ready to eat."

Storey spun, horrified. "What?"

"Kidding," he muttered. "I think they want us to move."

He backed up closer to the water's edge, pulling Storey with him. Immediately the women poked them harder. Storey retreated more and the dark haired woman who'd been tormenting her, moved to the side and poked her more towards her back. "So do we go with them, or run across the water to the other side."

"I don't swim. Tammy probably doesn't swim. And we brought her here to find her people. How is running away going to help us?"

She hated when he was right. "Fine then."

Glaring at the woman poking her, Storey shifted her bag on her shoulders and grabbing Tammy's hand again, she nudged her in front so they could walk forward. Tammy walked but she wasn't happy. She kept an eye on the women and the tears looked like they'd fall at any time.

"Tammy is so not happy."

"And what can we learn from that?"

"That's she not overjoyed to see some of her people?"

Eric whispered, "I got that. The question is why?"

With the two women now bringing up the rear of their little group, they walked for close to fifteen minutes. She was itching to drag out one of her portals and escape to Paxton's lab. Except, Eric was right. They'd come here to find Tammy's people. And they'd found them.

Only no one appeared to be happy about it.

Eric's words echoed her thoughts. "We don't know for sure that Tammy is wanted here."

She gulped. "Surely, anyone would be devastated to lose a child."

They kept walking forward. Storey's eyes searched from one side to the other. There was no sign of other Louers. No possessions. No buildings. No activity.

"Maybe, maybe not. They can't have it easy yet and Tammy is just another mouth to feed."

"So do we take her home again?"

"Your home or my home? You know how my people feel. We only have to consider Jendron's face when he saw her to understand that. Fear does that to a society."

"I don't know how my people would treat her. But it would be almost impossible to keep her secret. I'd have the government down on me in days. I'm sure her DNA would prove to be very different. That alone would make the scientists want to keep her under observation. What kind of life is that for her?"

"Not much of one. So forward we go then. For better or worse."

ERIC DIDN'T LIKE any of their options. How many Louers were actually here? He had no way of knowing. What bothered him was Tammy's reaction. It's obvious the women frightened her, but why? Had she bonded too long and too hard with Storey that she didn't want to go back to her old life? Was she afraid of being punished for having run off and being left behind?

As with everything of late, there were more questions than answers. Why did parents play such a prominent role in their current difficulties? He had no idea where his own father had gone or what he could be up to. Then there was the problem of Storey's parents. Maybe they could find Tammy's parents and solve at least one problem.

Of course not.

Shepherded as they were, Storey didn't realize they'd arrived at their destination until they were suddenly surrounded by a large group of Louers. She stiffened as a large, angry looking male approached. *Oh shit.* "Eric, look at his arm."

Eric stiffened. The Louer wore a series of numbers on his arm. "Not good."

Surreptitiously, she grabbed one of the sheets of paper with a portal on it to take them back to Paxton's lab. "I don't know about you, but escape is starting to look like a good idea.”

"You and me both.”

Some of the younger members of the group reached out to touch Storey's long hair. Her bag was grabbed. She jerked it free, glaring at the offenders. "That's enough.”

She nudged Tammy forward so everyone could see she had a Louer child with her.

Silence.

Tammy stared at them, her fingers clenching hard on Storey's hand. "Why does no one seem happy to see her?”

"I don't know.” Eric held the note and slowly pivoted, showing it to everyone in the group.

"We didn't consider that there could be several different groups of Louers from the one complex. It's possible her family is in another totally different area.”

"Then what do we do?” She despaired of finding an answer.

Just then a cry went up from the other side of the group. Tammy opened her mouth and an answering cry came from her.

Eric and Storey exchanged glances. "Now we're getting somewhere.”

A smaller built Louer female squeezed in front of the crowd. She jumped up and down, her sturdy body vibrating in excitement. For the first time, Tammy dropped Storey's hand and ran over to the new arrival.

"Family or friend?” Storey asked in a low murmur.

"Don't know.”

More Louers arrived from the same direction. What fascinated Storey was the sheer lack of expression on the faces of the others in the group. As if they were completely unaffected by the scene playing out in front of them. They continued to watch Storey and Eric. As if nothing else mattered. Storey also had the weird sensation of a low buzz going on in the ethers around them. Telepathic communication maybe?

Even the new arrivals failed to show any emotion. Storey hated it. Tammy had been through a lot and she'd done it with remarkable calm. Now she knew why. She'd learned from her elders.

Storey and Eric turned slowly as if to check out their surroundings, but were in fact wondering if they were knee deep in Louers on all sides. The answer was yes.

Storey sighed. "Suggestions?"

"We could run for it. Tammy has found someone to be with. Whether they are her parents isn't the issue. She's found someone who can help her more than we can at this point."

"So on the count of three, we run back toward the river and pop through a portal?"

Relief showed on his face. "Sounds good."

She grinned. "Can we find a way to get through this wall though? Or do we try to open a portal here and disappear without any of them jumping in too?"

Eric searched around. "We barely have room to open it. I say break through the line to the left."

Trying not to be too obvious, Storey checked out where Eric had mentioned. There were only a couple of Louers on that side with a space between them. She could go low and Eric could probably just bolt through.

"One, two and three…"

The blow came out of nowhere. Exploding on the side of her head like it did, she barely saw Eric crumpling to the ground as the ground rushed to meet her. A horrible cry erupted from Tammy.

Storey's cheek bounced twice on the ground then the world went black.

ERIC WOKE SLOWLY, his head pounding in agony. Bright sunlight beat down on his poor eyes, making it hard to open them. He gulped the fresh air, grateful it was not the stinky fumes of the Louers' old home.

After another moment, trying to remember where he was, he attempted to roll over. An explosion went off inside his head. He collapsed backwards. Getting his next breath became a challenge. Finally he succeeded, somewhere around the same time the pain became manageable.

He drew on his ranger training to try and assess the damage. Aching pain in the head, but...the rest of him appeared to be fine.

"Storey?"

No answer. With that the memories came rushing back.

Please let her be here. He did not want to have to chase around this dimension looking for her. And he wouldn't leave without her. With one, then a second deep breath, he rolled over slightly, this time managing the movement with minimal pain. With his eyes out of the direct sun, he tried opening them again. All he could see was bare ground. Casting his gaze while lying immobile he saw a line of trees further out. No guard within sight. Was he contained in any way? Or had he been left for dead? Any minute now, he'd grab his courage and try to stand up.

Now.

With uncoordinated movements, he made it onto his butt. Immediately he buried his head in his hands as the pounding took over. A head injury wouldn't do this, would it? Had they injected him with something? A drug of some kind? He had no idea what weapons the Louers had at their disposal, but whatever they'd used, it had brutal side effects.

Taking several shallow breaths, he finally lifted his head and looked around. He was alone. Left behind? Left for dead? Unwanted? Of no value? Relief mixed with worry and both were ringed with unaccountable anger. They'd taken Storey with them and had dumped him where he'd stood.

Unimportant, irrelevant, discarded.

Well, he'd see about that. First though, he had to check out what shape he was in. Giving his body a quick going over, he realized he was uninjured. That was the good news. The bad news was his codex was gone. As were the portals that Storey had insisted he stash in his pockets in case she lost hers or in case they were separated.

He had no way to communicate. No way to go home. And no way to escape.

Crap.

The loss of his codex bothered him. It was a part of him. A tool, but one that was also a lifeline to his home.

He felt naked without it. And lost.

STOREY CAME TO full wakefulness in a flash. She didn't move, instinct telling her she was in a new, unknown place. Her brain struggled to sort out what her eyes were seeing. She appeared to be in a small cave. *Again a cave.* The fresh smell reassured her she hadn't ended up back in the Louers' dimension. The top of the small space rose less than a dozen feet above her head. Light shone from the side, but in pale, weak rays.

There wasn't a sound. No Louers, no running water, no

wind whispering through the trees. Silence filled the space, making it uncomfortable as anxiety filled the emptiness. And what about Eric? Was Tammy okay?

What about her stylus? Her hand slapped against her chest. Panic threatened to cut off her airways. Then she found it. The stylus was caught against the band of her bra. *Oh thank God.*

With the stylus, she had hope.

She rolled to the right and pushed onto her elbow to look around. Nothing and no one. The back of the cave stretched only a few feet behind her, offering nothing but more dirt and rock. Light shone in from the mouth of the cave.

With that, she did a personal assessment. She felt no physical pain and although stiff, she could move everything. Still, her codex was missing. Her backpack was missing. And her pockets appeared to have been emptied. Damn, she could use a granola bar right about now. And paper. Crap. All her paper was gone. Every pocket she'd manage to stuff a piece of paper in had been cleaned out. She groaned. Her stylus and no paper. Figured.

Well, she'd been there before.

Or…maybe not. She checked her bra. A silent woot went through her brain. She had one piece of paper still hidden.

Now where the hell had Eric gotten to?

Damn.

The entrance of the cave beckoned. Was she a prisoner? Was she even still in the same dimension? She peered around the edge of the rock face. Another big meadow. Trees. Blue sky and sunshine.

And no sign of Eric or the Louers.

Bouncing on her toes, her breath caught and held. Her blood pulsing with fear, she mentally counted down. Three, two, one… She bolted for the trees.

And made it to the cover of the first couple of evergreens. She hid behind the largest trunk and caught her breath. Still, no sign of anyone.

She studied the geographical area. The trees made it difficult to get a decent look. She needed to get higher. A large spruce tree with huge hanging boughs offered both protection and height. Seconds later, she'd slipped under the waist high branches and had a leg up on the next branch. Ignoring the stinging in her palms as the bark scraped her hands, she climbed from one branch to the next. Finally she made it close to the top, or at least high enough that she could look over the meadow and valley.

Cliffs dotted a large mountain off to the left. Hollows on the side of the open faces reminded her of New Mexico and the cliff dwelling homes of the Anasazi people. She hadn't visited them herself but had studied it in school. A perfect spot for the Louers.

As she searched the area, she tried to find the river where they'd first met the female Louers. Maybe that was the shine off to the right. She was relatively safe up here and found herself relaxing to the point of taking her time and studying the area. It was almost familiar. Almost. Something about it though… Back home there'd been a place where she and her mom had often picnicked. She didn't have the same cliffs off to the side though so obviously it wasn't the exact location, yet it had the same effect of making her homesick.

Small towns like the one she'd grown up in, rivers, creeks and climbing trees were just a way of life. Being out here didn't make her nervous. It made her comfortable. Free in a way.

She hoped Eric felt the same way.

ERIC STUMBLED FORWARD, wishing his head would stop screaming at him. His stomach had already emptied once. His mouth would love a good rinse and his dry throat needed a drink.

He'd searched the area and there was no sign of anyone. The meadows and trees seemed to continue forever. Storey might struggle with all this openness being a small town girl. Unlike him. He was a ranger and was used to tough conditions. She was a schoolgirl without his training to fall back on. This couldn't be easy on her. On the other hand, she might be treated as a princess returning the lost daughter, enjoying a hot meal and a good rest.

Unlike him.

They'd emptied all his pockets. Too bad, he could use one of Storey's unending granola bars about now.

Why was there so much dratted country here? No buildings, no roads, no signs of civilization at all. How long would it take the Louers to build? Or would they live in caves? Make treehouses, or build structures of some kind? Was he to watch the ground for dugout type buildings, like into the side of a hill? Or could they throw up something instantly with a technology he had yet to hear about?

He had no idea. His people had technology that made building a relatively easy task. However, his people didn't do anything fast. They took, like Storey had once pointed out, a long time to make any decision. Therefore, although her people might need time to do the actual construction manually, they probably still completed their projects before his people, who could take years to determine and discuss the type, purpose, location, and size. It didn't take long once a decision was made, months maybe, but the decision making took years. Sad really.

And his people thought they were so advanced, so much better than the inhabitants of the other two dimensions. A thought that made him cringe as he remembered his dimensional lessons. Her world was always held up as an example of overpopulation, warmongering and power hungry politicians. Her world was theirs without controls, without regulations and with way too many people.

Everything was perspective.

Chapter 11

STOREY LEANED BACK against the trunk of the tree, grateful for the vantage point and somewhat safe position. Most people didn't think to look up when searching for something and she didn't think she could be seen from where she sat. All she needed now was Eric.

Settling back against the tree a little more securely, she pulled her stylus out from her shirt. Undoing the strap she'd used to tie it around her neck, she immediately felt the hum on her hand as the stylus woke.

"Hey, Stylus," she said, feeling a little odd without paper in her hand. "I have almost no paper to write your answers, so if there is another way to do this, now would be a good time to learn." Her hand slapped down on her jean leg. Immediately the words shone on her jean material.

Can write on anything.

"Good. That's excellent. Where is Eric?"

Walking.

"Alone?"

Yes.

"Close by?"

Yes.

"Where are the Louers?"

Hidden.

"Why?"

Scared.

"Is Tammy okay?"

Yes.

"Good. Then I can find Eric and go home. Right?"

Right.

Now she was feeling better. Except she didn't feel totally better. She stared down at her pant leg and realized she'd run out of space soon.

"Is Tammy with her family?"

No.

"No? Where is she then?"

With the Louers.

"Why not with her family?"

Her family isn't here.

Oh shit. That wasn't good. "They will they take her to her family, right?"

No.

She closed her eyes, her stomach churning with fear. "Why not?"

Tammy is the daughter of the leader of the Louers, but has been taken prisoner by this small offshoot group.

Oh shit. "Is she hurt?"

She's unharmed.

Right, to the stylus it was the same thing. Not to her though. "Is Tammy close by?"

Yes.

"Do we need to help her get to her family?" No answer.

What was she to do with that? Then again, the stylus couldn't make decisions for her… "I don't understand what these Louers want with Tammy?"

She's to be sacrificed if her father won't step down. Not all the Louers are happy about being in this dimension. With the portal damaged, they are cut off from the others and their means to survive. They can't go home. They are scared.

Home. Back to that dark, cold place. Yuck, but then it's all they knew. "And Tammy's father? What does he want?"

He wants to stay and build here. Says it is a better place. The others want to force him to make a new portal so they can go back.

And this is where the problem lies. With a sinking heart, she said, "Only…he can't create a portal, can he?"

No.

So if he doesn't make one, they'd sacrifice Tammy. Not nice. "Why Tammy?"

Because they recognized her. As they hate him, they also hate her. So she's become a weapon to be used.

Double not nice. Who'd have thought the Louers would have dissident groups, too? "Why did the second group come over if they didn't like it?"

They thought it would be better, but to them it isn't.

"What do they want?"

Food, housing, the things they are used to.

That was understandable. Change was hard on everyone. Change without the means to adapt to their new place would be almost impossible. "So what can I do now?"

Find Eric, then find a way to go home and stay there, or help Tammy return to her people and find a way to make the Louers happy.

She groaned. "Make it easy, why don't you. How can I possibly make them happy? I already made this dimension for them, surely that's enough."

No. They need a portal so they can go back and forth and bring equipment over to help them grow food and build their buildings.

"So if I build them a portal, will that make them happy?"

The stylus hummed. *Maybe.*

Maybe? She groaned louder. "That's hardly good enough. With a portal they can have some people living on both sides of the dimension. Then travel as they want to and have the best of both worlds."

But Storey knew the truth. People were people no matter the dimension. Never happy.

First thing first. Find Eric.

ERIC KEPT PUTTING one foot in front of the other. It's not like there were many options. He had to find Storey. With any luck she had the means to get them back home. It would be a long time before he'd be willing to come back to either of the Louer dimensions. He could only hope that Tammy and Skorky were with her parents.

Speaking of parents, and fathers in particular, where had his gone? His father might have gone into hiding. But where? And why? It's not as if he could hide out forever. At one point, he'd have to face the Council. Unless he hoped the issues would die down.

But they wouldn't. At least not while Eric was still fighting for Storey's side.

He studied the dry ground, green, tall grasses waving slowly in the breeze and the tree branches bouncing gently higher up. The tall treetops swayed gently. From the database on Storey's world, he'd read about people who built houses in trees. There'd even been movies of some of Storey's people playing in trees, kids climbing them, playing games in and around them. An odd, but fascinating concept. He'd never climbed a tree in his life.

His survival training had pointed out the advantages of getting to the top and having a better view of the area, but there were distinct disadvantages as well. Like being trapped and surrounded by the enemy.

Then there was the actual physical attempt to climb one. He studied a large tree at his side. The first branches were above his jumping height. His training had included running, portal hopping, cliff jumping, rope work, communications, but as he looked around the woods, he understood there hadn't been enough wilderness training. He frowned, for the first time realizing how inadequate his training actually had been. In fact, when compared to some of what Storey's people went through, his had been a joke.

His people had never experienced war, never before been invaded and had never contemplated not being at the top of the food chain – a Storey phrase that seemed even more appropriate at this time.

His gaze went from treetop to treetop, shaking his head. There. His gaze caught on something as it went past. He returned to studying it, grateful his eyes were good enough to catch the slight movement.

Catch it but not understand it. He slipped around behind the trees and crept closer. That was another thing he had yet to see here, animals, wildlife of any kind. Storey felt she'd made a complete copy of her world, but had she included the animal world in that vision? An ecosystem of insects. Had she even thought to consider removing the human element here or was that another worry they needed to consider?

He crept a little closer.

And came to a dead stop.

It was Storey.

Sitting at the top of the tree, enjoying the sunshine – for all the world as if she had no worries. Relief and frustration whipped through him. Why did she always end up on top?

"Storey?"

She didn't notice. Dare he yell at her and alert anyone around to their presence? Well, he wasn't going to climb the tree after her. So…he opened his mouth and yelled, "Storey!"

Now he'd caught her attention. She waved madly at him. He laughed. Everything she did, she did with enthusiasm. He loved that about her. As he watched, she disappeared from view. The top of the tree swayed and wiggled under his fascinated gaze as she descended the tree like a pro.

Next thing he knew, she slipped out from under the lower boughs and was running toward him.

And straight into his arms.

STOREY LAUGHED AS Eric snatched her off the ground and swung her around. Finally, she pulled back enough to say, "It's so good to see you. You collapsed in front of me and then everything went dark. When I woke up, there was no sign of you."

"You saw me collapse? Did they hit me or something?" He reached up to rub his temple. "I've had this horrible headache since I woke up."

"I didn't see anything. Although I did hear Tammy scream. I've been worried. Have you seen her at all?"

"I haven't seen anyone." He wrapped her in a second tight hug before setting her away from him, his face grim.

"While I was out, they took everything I had on me. Even my codex." He held out his bare arm for her to see.

"Me too." She showed him her am. "They also took all my paper, my backpack, all the food. But…" She shot him a huge beaming smile. "They didn't get my stylus or one sheet of paper"

He groaned with relief and raised his gaze skyward in relief. "Thank heavens for that."

"But," she cautioned him, "I don't know how to make a portal. The paper is small. I'm not sure how to make it work."

He frowned. "So close but we're not quite there. That's okay, Tammy is back with her people, so mission accomplished there."

"Um, yeah that might be a problem." She stopped and shifted her feet restlessly, her gaze wandering the treed area. How did she tell him about Tammy? "You're right about a couple of things. The stylus does appear to be working well and with its help I'm sure we can figure out how to get home."

Relief washed over his face. "When you started to speak I was sure you were going to say something I wasn't going to like."

"I am." She winced, took a deep breath and explained what the stylus had said.

"What?" His outrage rippled through the trees. She just didn't know if it was outrage for poor Tammy or for her unspoken suggestion that they rescue her. "Also consider the codexes. Do you want to leave them here? Mine is supposed to allow me to get back to your dimension without much knowledge of how to use it…" she let her voice trail off as his eyes widened in horror.

"You don't think they would use it to go to my world?" The color drained from his face.

She didn't know how to answer. "Do you want to leave that as an option. I'm pretty sure no one in your dimension will be pleased if we return without them."

Eric stared at her, resignation and acceptance slowly making its way into his gaze. "I really didn't want to hear that. But there's no way I can leave my world vulnerable to another attack."

Soberly she answered. "And there's no way I can leave Tammy in danger either."

"Oh no."

"I'm sorry. But I can't. We brought her over here. For a chance at life. Not to ensure her death." Her pleading look was impossible to ignore. And he cared too much about her to ignore it. This mattered to her. And if he was honest, he'd have a hard time walking away and leaving Tammy to her fate. Now the rodent, yeah, that one he could leave behind. He'd never understood why anyone would have such a creature as a pet. That she had a pet at all showed a socializing structure he'd never have given the Louers credit for.

"No, we can't." Standing back, he considered the issue. The two of them obviously weren't considered a threat as they'd been left behind with no guard to keep an eye on them.

They would be able to find the Louers, most likely. However, locating Tammy, sneaking her away and finding her family was an entirely different matter. He reached up and rubbed the back of his neck.

"I saw caves in a hillside up ahead." Storey suggested

helpfully. "Some of my ancient people lived in similar abodes. It's possible they've taken cover there." She pointed toward the north. "It's just a short walk."

Eric studied the area, nodded decisively then reached out and snagged her hand.

He smiled down at her. "I don't want to get separated again," he said. "So don't mind if I just hang on tight for awhile."

She squeezed his hand tight. "My sentiments exactly."

They walked in casual silence for several minutes.

"I wonder why I was left in a cave?" She looked at him. "Where were you?"

"I'm presuming I woke where I fell. It was a meadow similar to where I remember being when we walked as a group."

"Odd. They left you where you fell, and they carried me off and left me free to leave when I woke up." She shrugged. "Why?"

"Maybe they thought you had value and then changed their minds. Or maybe they thought we died and should be left behind. Who knows?"

"I wonder how big this group of Louers is." Storey had been trying to figure that out. "The stylus told me about the Louers plans for Tammy."

"And how would it know?"

"He was a Louer, once. I presume he's got a way to tap into what they are thinking. Although it would be best if we find out for sure."

A few minutes later, hiding behind a tree and using her pant leg to write on, she asked the stylus how he'd known.

I heard them speak of it.

Storey sat back on her heels. "Of course. Just because I

was unconscious doesn't mean that the stylus was sleeping. It would have heard everything going on. And being Louer it understood the language clearly."

She tucked the stylus back under her shirt. "Let's go. We need to make sure they don't have time to put their plan into action."

The sun shone hot in the meadow, but the shade provided by the many trees along the edge of the field gave some relief. Eric didn't recognize many of the tree species. The sheer variety of colors and types was fascinating. Brilliant. They came to the edge of the woods and stared.

Across from the meadow stood a high cliff dotted with black caves.

Eric pulled her back behind the trees.

"Look."

STOREY PEERED AROUND the pine tree in the direction Eric had pointed out. She spotted movement by the caves. There seemed to be almost pathways between the caves. As she watched someone walked from one to the other. She hunkered down low. "Eric, are they Louers?"

"Who else would they be?"

"I don't know. I'd just like to make sure."

"No way to do that from here." He motioned to a large clump of trees that butted up against the base of the cliff edge closest to them. "Let's sneak over there."

Following his lead, they slipped from tree to tree, then raced as fast as they could through the open area to the relative safety of the shadows once again. Gasping for breath, Storey bent over trying to calm down. "That was fun. Not."

A strangled laugh escaped Eric as he watched her. He

wasn't short of breath, she noted sourly. But he'd been cool and calm throughout this whole event. Unlike her, who'd gone from one extreme to the other.

Still, they were close now. She could see and feel it. Tammy would be hidden in one of those spots, maybe guarded and maybe not. The adult Louers wouldn't see her as a danger or in danger of running off. In fact, they'd probably have ignored her the whole time. They'd be more interested in the items they'd stolen from Eric and her. Especially if they understood what they'd found. Tammy would show them if given a chance.

If not, well, they might be able reclaim some of it.

"Do we have a plan of action?" she asked, hoping he'd figured out what to do from here. She didn't think the stylus would be much help. At this point, she couldn't see a way to use it effectively.

"I wish we knew where Tammy was stashed. That info would help to find a way to sneak her out. As it is, they can see us as soon as we move. There's no cover. They've got a heck of a location here." His admiring tone made her turn to look at him.

"What? They do." He said defensively, "It's easy to defend and offers maximum protection."

She studied the layout. "It didn't help my people. They died out almost overnight."

"From what?"

"Who knows? They lived well for a long time, centuries I think, then they all disappeared. It's one of the great mysteries of my people." From the confusion on his face, she could see that didn't make any sense. This wasn't the time for a history lesson on the Anasazi people, especially since she had no answers. "Don't worry about it. I'll explain when we have more time."

He turned back to study the cave structure. "You know, if these caves go to the ground level, we might be able to gain access."

"I don't think they do. The whole point of living in caves like this is safety. To allow access from down here is to leave a door open for intruders."

"Were all your people about fighting and war? Surely it would make sense to have access for things like hunting and water."

"Yes," she said slowly, "but I wouldn't count on it."

He rolled his eyes and rubbed the bridge of his nose. "So…now what? We could go to the cliffs above them and try to climb down or we could climb up from here and hope we're not seen."

Storey studied the area more intently. "They had to have carried Tammy up there. I can't see her climbing that high on her own."

"That wouldn't have been hard. They're a large, strong people and she's a child to them. It would be natural for them to carry her."

"True." And that shot her idea down. Not that it had been much of an idea. There had to be a way to get to the first cave, which presumably was connected to the others inside the cliff.

She studied the cliff wall at her side. There were no cut-in steps on the face of the wall that she could see, but there must be some somewhere. They'd be hard to spot unless you knew of them. Hard to climb, unless you knew how. The best way to find them would probably be to walk along the ground, hands on the rock face, hoping to come across them by feel. She doubted they'd be easy to see otherwise.

It was afternoon, at least the sun was high and fairly warm. They couldn't wait that long for the sun to go down. Tammy was in trouble and…so were they.

Giving Eric a quick explanation, she slipped through the trees until she was as close as she could get to the cliff. She chose the first outcropping of rock, hoping it partially hid her from above. Checking the cliff wall carefully for Louers patrolling the top, she darted to the projection of rock and flattened against the cold stone. And froze. Did she hear something?

From the corner of her eye she could see Eric hiding in the trees. He gave her a smile. Okay. She'd made it. Relief rippled down her back.

The cliff appeared pockmarked like a lava rock but not as porous. Parts of the rock were smooth, others sharp. Varied in color and texture, the rock reminded her of the southwestern part of the States. Interesting.

She moved silently along the rock face, hugging the wall. In a moment, Eric joined her. Unless someone stood outside and stared straight down, they wouldn't be seen. They kept it up for another fifty odd feet when she stopped. Leaning her head close to the wall, she saw a pattern in the rock.

Could it be that easy? The pattern started at the rock ahead. Interesting. After giving her eyes a few moments to adjust to the multiple colors, she saw the beginning of the steps. With just a couple of steps, she'd climbed a good ten feet upwards. She heard Eric's gasp of surprise but kept going, knowing they were vulnerable on the open rock face. Besides he'd be following on her heels.

If anyone approached the caves from the woods or meadow as she and Eric had, they'd be spotted immediately. With that thought, she grabbed her courage and ran up the hidden staircase. Knowing Eric would be right behind her, she made it to the lowest plateau, where the first of the caves started. Ducking out of sight into the first cave, she gasped for air. Her heart slammed against her ribcage. She hated this. They could be found out any moment.

Eric joined her in seconds. The cave was huge. And empty.

They looked at each other. "I wonder if they're connected?" she whispered.

Knowing they could be found any time, they explored the caves with an eye to finding their way through the labyrinth of tunnels. The entire bottom row of caves appeared empty. There were connecting passages, and Storey couldn't believe how spacious the area appeared. If the weather stayed warm, the new inhabitants might actually have a cool place to live, temporarily or permanently. She thought it would be fun to spend a summer here.

But not with the Louers.

At the last cave on that level, noises finally penetrated the silence. Someone was close by. Working their way quietly through the tunnels, they tracked the noise deep within the cliff. Darkness shadowed the area. Maybe that worked in their favor too.

Walking slowly in the dark, the noise finally became recognizable. "That has to be Tammy."

"Or another child?"

"No." Storey knew that voice already like she knew her own voice. The noise was horrible. And Storey had nothing to give her to keep her quiet and happy. Damn. No one appeared to be rushing to keep her quiet either.

With the noise at an all-time high, Storey stuck her head around the corner of the last wall. Tammy, still wearing

Storey's t-shirt, lay curled in the far corner. Alone.

Storey motioned at Eric to take a look. As she took a second look, Tammy's pet poked its head out from her arms and saw them. It raced toward Storey chattering in a loud voice. It still wore the harness and had a lead attached. Even as they watched, the rodent hit the end of the lead at full power and snapped back. It was enough to shake Tammy out of her crying jag. She sat up, and for the first time, Storey saw tear tracks on the little girl's cheeks. Tammy looked toward them, but Storey thought the girl probably couldn't see them in the dark cave. Storey took a step closer so her outline separated from the wall.

Tammy stared, her mouth dropped open as if to start screaming again. Storey slapped her hands over her ears in preparation. Instead Tammy scrambled to her feet and ran toward her. Eric stepped up beside Storey and grinned. Tammy opened her arms and launched herself at them both.

It almost took both of them to stop her assault. Still, for all her excitement and happiness at seeing them again, she was silent.

A wonderful blessing. Tammy squeezed hard, her arms wrapped around both of their necks in a group hug that Eric and Storey couldn't possibly escape. Eric spluttered several times. Storey looked over and started to laugh silently. She didn't dare make a sound, but it was hard to stay quiet. Skorky was jumping on Eric's head. Obviously he was happy to see them too.

Untangling herself from Tammy's arms, Storey walked over quickly to where Tammy had been lying on the ground, hoping some of her supplies might be there. There was nothing. *Damn.* Just one more break – that's all they needed – one lousy break and they'd be gone.

Back to Paxton. Back to her home. Anywhere was better than here.

"Storey." Eric's hoarse whisper had her walking quickly back to them.

"What?"

"Look." He held up a folded piece of paper. "This was in Tammy's pocket."

Excitement raced through her. Storey opened it up. "It's a portal to my house."

"Let's go." He almost jumped with impatience. "Just spread it out and I'll go through now. I think I hear someone coming. It's probably because she quit wailing."

Storey laid the portal on the cave floor. She didn't know if the dense rock would affect the portal's function or not. They didn't have much choice. They'd have to try it. As soon as she had the paper spread out properly, Eric, Tammy and the rodent still in his arms, stepped through and disappeared.

A loud shout sounded from the shadows. Shit. They were out of time. She snatched up the corner of the paper and jumped, making sure she took the drawing through with her. The last thing she saw were two of the big Louers coming out of the shadows.

CHAPTER 12

"**S**HIT."

Muffled groans and an odd shriek greeted her softer than expected landing. Tammy and Eric had cushioned her fall. She didn't even want to contemplate having squished the skorl. She scrambled to her feet and turned around, frowning. It looked like her dimension – sort of. If you expected to arrive in a storeroom of some kind.

At least they were alone.

"Where the hell are we?" Eric sat on the cement floor and stared.

Storey wished she had some idea. "It should have been my house, but…" she pivoted slowly, staring, "apparently not."

Eric hopped to his feet. "Oh great."

His voice sounded so disgusted and pissed; she fell immediately into apologizing. "Well, I'm sorry. I didn't exactly plan this. I don't know if something happened to the portal. Maybe they did something to it and gave it back to her, hoping we'd use it."

He spun around, astonishment on his face. "I'm not criticizing you. I'm simply wishing that for once things would go our way."

She waited a long moment for them both to calm down. "We could look on this turn of events as having gone very well." She let him consider that. "Just think, we snuck in, grabbed Tammy, and escaped – unscathed. Personally, I'd consider that things *are* going our way."

He shot her a frustrated look. "I know. It just seems like we go one step forward but then two steps backwards. Why? Why couldn't we have landed in your bedroom or Paxton's lab? Why here?" He gestured to the inside of a large empty room they were in.

"Why not here?" she laughed. "Okay, I know this isn't where we want to be, but it is much better than where we were."

Tammy made an odd sound, almost a prelude to her wailing. Both of them started. "Please not." Storey had nothing to appease her with if she started screaming. She walked over and hugged her. "It is okay, Tammy. We'll be fine."

"Will we?" murmured Eric. She shot him a warning look, nodding at Tammy.

He rolled his eyes at her. But restated in a perkier voice, "We will."

Tammy's lower lip trembled but the wailing appeared to have been averted for the moment, as if she understood what they were saying.

Keeping a hand on Tammy's shoulders, Storey stood up. "Good. Now, can we see about going home?"

Tammy looked up expectantly at both of them. Storey pointed at the door. "Let's see what's out there." Together the three of them trooped to the door. Eric pulled it open.

Outside, daylight shone bright and clear. Storey stepped out first. They appeared to be in a commercial storage unit where people could store their personal belongings. A couple of older trucks were parked outside the smaller sheds at the far end.

Storey searched the horizon for landmarks. Something to identify where they were. Casually, they walked through the front gates, not drawing any attention or curious glances. In fact, they were pretty much ignored. That worked for her.

Outside she found a sidewalk traveling in both directions on an average looking street. It could be any small town in North America. Or, it could be a street in Eric's dimension for all she knew – having never seen any.

A large blue pickup drove past, reaffirming her assumption that they were in her dimension. Tammy squealed at the noise, her arms wrapping tight about Storey. Right. This was probably the first time the child had seen anything even close to this. Storey hugged her tight for a long moment. Murmuring comforting words, she took a firm hold on Tammy's hand and led her forward.

Inside, her heart leapt with joy. This resembled home. Even that mountain in the distance looked familiar. A little different because of the angle but so close, she wanted to jump for joy. Ahead was a standard streetlight. She had to be home.

Maybe not home-home, but somewhere close. At least she hoped so. Even the street signs looked normal. They stopped at the corner of Main and Collingwood. That was an intersection in her town of Bankhead, but not an area she knew well.

"We'll go this way." She motioned toward Main Street.

"Do you know where we are?" Eric asked, staring at the lights and signs in confusion.

Glancing around again, she said, "I can't be sure yet, but I think we're in my home town."

Eric laughed. "This is nothing like your home."

She grinned at him. "You've only seen my house, the school, the mine and pathways in between. This could be the other side of town where the mill is. I don't spend a lot of time over here, so I'm not exactly sure yet. We need to keep walking so I can recognize more landmarks."

"Like those mountains?" He pointed to several snow capped peaks off the left.

"Yes, exactly like those." They walked in companionable silence for the rest of the block. Tammy never made a sound but her eyes were huge as she tried to take it all in. Her head swiveled from side to side. For her, this had to be a huge shock, but she was handling it well. Eric appeared to take it all in stride.

"Do you have towns like this, Eric?"

"Not like this." He grinned as an old van rattled by, large painted flowers in bright colors decorating its sides. "Definitely not like this."

She had to laugh. The next block was Cantor Street. Yes. Now that one she'd heard of for sure. She had to be several miles from home. She had to orient herself. The recreation center was over a couple of blocks and behind that was a trail to the high school. That would be the fastest way. With more energy in her step than she'd felt so far, she led them through the back way to her house.

Tammy stumbled. Eric reached out and helped her to regain her footing. Storey stopped to check her over. Tammy had to be getting tired. She'd been incredibly strong and valiant but at this point she needed food and rest. "We're almost home, Tammy. Just a little further. There should be food when we get there." Although what she had no idea; they'd wiped out so much food the last time. Had her mother had time to restock? Would she have gone out and replaced it? Or would she be waiting, pissed off, for Storey to come home?

Her house loomed ahead. Thank heaven for that. Luckily, she couldn't see the vehicle parked out front.

They walked to the back door of the kitchen. The door was locked.

Storey's switched her gaze from the closed door and back to him in amazement. "Really? We never lock our door."

"Yet, someone stole a whole pile of food while they were out one time, so I guess it makes sense that they'd lock it now?" Eric's sardonic humor had her grinning.

"Okay, fine. I'll run around and check the front door. Stay here."

Giving Tammy a quick reassuring grin, she ran around the house to the front door. It too was locked. Oh hell. She tried the garage. The inside looked different. Having a father around all the time could account for that. There were tools, shelves and cans of paint stacked in one corner. The inside door was unlocked.

Yes. She pushed it open and ran to the back door, opening it for Tammy and Eric. Ushering them inside, she said, "Take her to my room, quickly in case they come home. I'll look for something to eat."

Eric nodded, grabbed Tammy's hand and led her to the stairs. "Don't be long. She looks ready to pass out."

Storey cast a worried glance at Tammy. Her normal robust color was long gone and her shoulders sagged. Even her eyes drooped. Yet she'd been a trooper throughout all this.

"I'll be quick." Giving them an encouraging smile, she disappeared into the kitchen. The table was different. She hated the nervous energy bubbling in her stomach. She could only hope her mother was happier in this reality than she'd been in the other one. Personally, Storey wanted the old one back. There was nothing wrong with the other table, damn it. She'd liked it.

The fridge had been restocked. At least one problem was solved. Under the sink was a garbage bag. Storey hauled out cheese and apples again. There was a quart of milk, she grabbed that. Ten minutes later, her bag was full and she was hauling it upstairs. The colors of the hallway were totally different. Gone was the overly bright baroque look. Instead there was a neutral beige covering the walls. Boring.

She walked into her room, turning and locking the door behind her.

And stopped.

This was her room.

But this was not *her* room. She didn't recognize anything in the room. There were no personal items, no pictures on the walls, no clothes in the closet. If this was her bedroom, everything had been cleaned out and removed.

She didn't live here anymore.

ERIC STUDIED THE look on Storey's face, the emotions whistling across her features faster than a north wind coming through the mountains. The bedroom had been almost dehumanized. Was this normal behavior when a child didn't return home? He'd hate to see Storey tossed from her home because of this. From what he'd seen, she'd been close to her mother. A relationship she'd valued.

The room looked so much the same, yet different. His gaze fell on Tammy, curled into a small ball and fast asleep on the bed. The bed that had different sheets and blankets on it. A similar bed, just dressed differently.

Her art books were missing and that could be a huge problem. She needed her paper. *They* needed her paper.

The stricken look on her face was hard to gaze upon. He busied himself poking into the closet, the same closet he'd hidden in earlier. Finally he heard her speak.

"The house is empty."

Her voice, low and intense, showed such control and balance, he couldn't help but admire her. Again. He didn't know that he could do the same if the conditions were reversed.

"And I have food."

Food. Such a mundane necessity given everything else that had come to pass.

"Thank you. Do you think we should let Tammy sleep?"

Storey gazed at the child, her features softening. His heart warmed. If nothing else, having someone else to look after helped her forget her own troubles. Some matters had to take precedence.

"Yes, she's exhausted. I can't believe how good she's been throughout this." Storey walked over to sit on the bed beside her. Grabbing the folded blanket at the foot of her bed, she gently covered Tammy up. "She's not complained once."

"No. She's been surprisingly easy so far." Eric sat in the middle of the floor. "I, however, could use something to eat."

She opened the bag she'd brought upstairs. "I grabbed what I could. It's not the same as last time, but close."

"Good. Is there cheese?"

He grinned when she held out a large block of white cheese, then another loaf of bread. "Tammy will be happy."

"That's if we leave her any." Storey sorted through the

food she'd brought. Eric made a simple sandwich and then watched her as he ate.

"Eric?"

He raised an eyebrow in question, his mouth full of food.

In a soft voice, Story asked. "What are we doing wrong? Everything seems to be getting worse."

STOREY COULDN'T HELP the wave of depression sweeping through her. Yes, they were warm and sheltered, with food at hand and they were safe from attacking Louers. But there were so many things wrong she couldn't begin to list them all.

Tammy's problem was the priority. How could she get Tammy home to her family? The stylus had at one time told her that she could delete the dimension she'd made but it would kill everyone in it. That meant all of Tammy's family and Tammy, if she were home at the time, would be wiped out. So not a good idea. She hadn't presented the idea to the Toran's because she'd figured they'd approve of the idea en masse. Getting rid of their enemy in one final drawing – yeah, they'd be all over that. Maybe not Eric, as he'd come to know Tammy.

They also had to go back and get the missing codexes. And her portals. She didn't like to think that one of them might jump into her bedroom. That made the hair on the back of her neck stand up straight.

"I'm thinking that maybe we should get Paxton's advice," Eric said.

She pondered that. "But we're no more welcome there than here."

"Did you ever consider that this…" he looked around, "might not be your room?"

The apple stalled midway to her mouth. "How do you mean?"

"What if we're in yet a different dimension? Or maybe a different time frame? Maybe your mother moved when you didn't return home."

Cold raced down her spine. She gasped in pain. "Oh, no way. I haven't been gone for that long."

"When you left the party, no. I don't know if time is the same here as there. It should be but…we've twisted so many things we can't count on it."

She slumped back from her position on the floor to lean against the bed. Her gaze centered on the pile of food, not really seeing it. "Why is it that when I try to help someone, the situation gets worse?"

He winced. "It doesn't always. Look, we rescued Tammy."

Storey sniffled, hating the image of that whole female weakness thing, but she'd love to break down and bawl – just for a moment. Just long enough to release the pressure valve threatening to blow. She'd feel so much better. But not here and not now – and not with Eric watching.

The apple would have to do. She took another bite. She needed the food for energy. The thought of this not being her home, or worse not being her dimension, made her sick. She loved her mother. For all her mother's foibles, they'd had a good relationship. They still did, she corrected herself mentally. There's no way she'd accept that her life with her mother was over.

"Ask the stylus." Eric gazed at her, one eyebrow raised.

"Good idea. But I'll need some paper."

"Would they have paper downstairs?"

She shrugged and stood up. "I don't know. I'll have to go see." She didn't want to leave the relative safety and quiet of the room, but she needed answers.

The master bedroom was at the end of the hall, right at the top of the stairs. Even if her parents or whoever lived here came home, it's possible that by keeping the light off in her room, no one would know they were hiding there. She could create another portal but all these jumps were taking them somewhere…not quite right…and she needed to find out why.

At her mom's room, she was forced to turn on the light. And stopped, swallowed hard, and quickly moved forward. Maybe her parents didn't live here. The bedroom set was a heavy mahogany with dark drapes and dark carpet. Terrible.

She strode to the night table and checked the drawers, hoping for a pad of paper. Nothing in the first drawer and the second one only offered a small note pad. Better than nothing, but she needed sheets of paper if her big sketchbooks weren't available. At this rate, she'd be leaving them in all the dimensions. If there was an office downstairs, then a printer and printer paper would be possible. Slipping down the stairs, keeping the lights off, she walked through the rooms, coming to the den. Half the room had been established as an office. Again dark furniture, dark carpets and even darker caramel walls. She hated it.

Walking to the computer, she saw it was still on but asleep. The monitor looked different, too. A great, big, square unit. As long as it worked. She booted it back out of hibernation then searched for paper. At the printer, she found a pile of perforated accordion paper that had gone out of style years ago. The printer also looked old, huge and clunky. Weird. Still the reams of paper were perfect and because it was continuous she could draw as big a picture as she needed too. Several inches should do.

Back at the computer, she opened a browser, and tried to bring up a few of her favorite sites to see if there were any messages. And couldn't find any of the pages. Her throat started to close in on her. Surely what she was thinking wasn't possible, was it? Clicking on the calendar in the corner of the screen, the day was May 21st and that was certainly reasonable, but the year – she gasped.

Ten years ago. Ten. A whole decade earlier than she wanted it to be. This wasn't her house. It wouldn't be her house for another few months at least. That's why it all looked so different. She didn't remember if this is how the house had looked when she first moved in because, well, she'd been a kid. So much hadn't happened yet. She'd only be in first grade. Chances were good her parents were either newly divorced or in the process. A tough time back then for her family.

Unbelievable.

Once again, her arms full, she ran up the stairs. Eric looked up in surprise as she burst into the room.

Trying to keep her voice low so as to not disturb Tammy, she said, "Oh Eric, we've got a bigger problem than we thought."

He frowned, grabbed an apple and took a big bite. "What are you talking about?"

"We've gone back in time. Ten years backwards."

His brows furrowed and he stopped chewing in mid bite. He blinked several times as if trying to process the information. "What? How do you know that?"

"The computer downstairs."

"Could it be wrong?"

Could it? She twisted her lips and considered. "I don't know. Maybe? I never thought to double check. God, that was stupid."

"Is there any way here to check? Without having to go downstairs again?"

How could they check? A small radio sat on the desk. A clock radio. She walked closer. "This might tell us." After pushing the power button, she set the dial to radio. Soft music filled the room. "I don't know if they'll talk about the date, though."

Along the back of the dresser sat an old calendar. For the year 2002. She picked it up, turning to show it to Eric. He frowned.

She scavenged through the rest of the drawers, wishing there'd be a few articles of usable clothing. Nothing. The closet was just as empty. Crap. The master bedroom might have some, but she had no way of knowing what size the woman, if there was a woman living here, wore. There might be a front closet with sweaters or jackets, but she and Tammy could use a change of clothes.

Striding to the center of the room, she dropped to the floor and reached for the ream of paper. Pulling out her stylus, she started in on the questions.

"Is it possible that we've gone back in time?"

A hum filled the air. *Yes.*

"Can we get back to our normal time?"

The answer came faster. *Yes.*

Her breath gusted out and she couldn't resist looking at Eric. He grinned. "See. We can fix this."

She rolled her eyes at him and returned to getting answers.

"Stylus, how do we go back to our time?"

Go back through the same portal.

"The portal that took us here? I thought it was damaged so we shouldn't use it again." She picked up the paper she'd folded and tossed at the foot of the bed.

When damaged they still go to the same place, but might not hit the target right on. In this case the time line appears to be damaged.

"Actually we ended up not quite in the right spot either. We were close, but landed several miles away."

Exactly.

Storey snickered. "To you maybe. So if we go to the same portal, we'll arrive either back outside of the house or inside this room again. And it could take us closer in time, or might hit the right time?

Yes.

"Oh boy."

Eric stood and looked at Tammy. "I could carry her."

"We could we end up miles away again."

He grimaced.

Storey continued to talk. "Stylus, if we try to go back to Paxton's lab, will the time frame be wrong there?"

Yes. You would be moving through this time frame now.

"So we have to fix the time here first?" She rubbed her eyes. When would something be simple.

That is correct.

"So after we get back to the normal time, how do we find Tammy's parents so that we can portal to them and reunite them? We don't want to go back and risk meeting the wrong group of Louers again."

Eric stepped up behind her to read the stylus message this time for himself. He crouched down, his arm over her shoulder.

"Hey, are you reading this?"

CHAPTER 13

ONE THING AT a time. Fix the time warp first.

Eric rubbed the back of his neck, his other hand absentmindedly rubbing Storey's back as he thought about what the stylus had written. Like it made something so hard to even contemplate – easy.

"I'm so tired. Do we rest first?" She stared at his face, so close to hers, for answers.

"Or do we do this next jump so that you are at least back in the house that you actually live in – at the right time."

She rolled her eyes. *Oh right.* "Yes, that makes sense. It would be wonderful if walking through that portal takes us right back into this room. Then we could sleep for a few hours."

On cue, they both looked over at the sleeping Tammy.

Storey frowned. "I hate to disturb her."

"If we're just going to end up back in this room, then I can pick her up, walk through and lay her back down again.

"Why is it I don't think it's going to be that simple?"

He grinned. "Because it never has been?" he suggested, straightening. He glanced around the room at the food still lying out in disarray. "I guess we should tidy this mess first."

"Definitely. It would be better to not leave any sign that we've been here."

"And I'm getting hungry again."

Storey groaned. "You're as bad as she is." She hopped to her feet and began cleaning up the food, absentmindedly making him another sandwich while she was at it. Bagging their food and garbage, she added the computer paper to their collection and put on her jacket. Finally, she laid the portal drawing on the floor. Glancing over at him, she watched as he carefully bent over Tammy and her pet, scooped them up like they hardly weighed anything. The skorl glared at him for disturbing his sleep but never cried out or tried to run off.

Straightening, Eric walked to where she stood. "Ready?"

Taking a deep breath, she said, "Yes." She stepped back as he hopped through, Tammy still asleep in his arms. He disappeared from sight.

"Please let this work."

She grabbed the corner and fell once more into the portal, taking the paper with her.

ERIC OPENED HIS eyes and studied his new location. It wasn't Storey's bedroom. Unfortunately. Tammy still slept in his arms and he'd have loved to have been able to lay her right back down. He waited for Storey to show up. And waited.

"Anytime Storey. I don't want to be lost in time without you and your portals, thank you very much."

The words had barely left his mouth when she arrived behind him.

She flopped back onto the pathway. In a hoarse whisper, she said, "I'd really like to be in bed right now."

"So would I." He waited a beat. "Any idea where we are?"

She groaned but staggered to her feet. "Not a clue." She brushed her pants off and straightened to look around her. "In theory, we should be closer to the house than last time."

"And we need to be because I won't be able to carry Tammy very far."

He shifted the load in his arms impatiently.

Determinedly, she spun around as if trying to orient herself. "Right then."

Eric watched the emotions flash across her face. Her face showed everything. She was so honest in her expression. There was no deceit. No subterfuge. You saw exactly what she was thinking. It also meant she couldn't lie to him.

A refreshing change. He didn't know many eligible women in his world and as a ranger, and worse, as the Councilman's son, he wasn't treated the same as the other guys. The women were more formal with him; more on the lookout for a long-term relationship instead of just a fun evening. In his world, he was considered a catch. He suspected Storey would laugh at that.

"Well," he prompted, hating to show he was tiring, but Tammy was a heavyweight. "I need to put Tammy down soon."

Storey spun around, a huge smile on her face. "I think I have it. Let's go." She took off ahead of him. He followed at a much slower pace. So much for believing he could do anything. The longer he carried Tammy, the more he realized he was going to need to bulk up his muscles if trips like this were to continue. As much as he hated the thought of not being invincible…

Then he saw it.

"Is that your house?" He looked around. "We came in from the other side." He brightened. "That's the path to the school where we first met, isn't it?"

"Yes, it is." She almost raced to the house, a lively bounce to her step.

"Storey, wait." He hated to blow her joy but someone needed to be the voice of reason here.

She spun around. "I'm sorry, what? I'm just so hoping this is it. That I'm home."

"I know that. But did you ever wonder if there might be another Storey in this house? In this dimension or this time?"

The smile fell off her face. Horror filled her gaze. "There couldn't be, could there?"

"I have no idea. It's just we're back at the same house, your house, supposedly in the time frame that you were living here back then…so where are you?"

She tilted her head back to stare up at the sky. "I'm getting a headache."

"And what's the chance the house is empty? Do we even know what day it is anymore? Are you in school today? Does your mother work? Did you consider any of that?"

"Of course, I didn't," she snapped. "I can't think straight anymore. But inside is a bed, my bed, where you can lay her down."

He considered that – for a heartbeat. "Right. Lead the way."

Again, she walked to the back kitchen door. He wondered why she never used the front door.

At the back, she found the kitchen door unlocked. "That's more like it."

"You aren't worried about intruders here?"

"No. Small town and all that." She pushed it open wide enough for him and Tammy to enter.

"Small town, two women who live a distance away from

any neighbors?"

"Let's just say that up to now, it hasn't been much of an issue."

He nodded, but doubted it would stay that way after life returned to normal. She'd changed. Become more self-confident. More secure. But with the confidence came more awareness of all the things that could go wrong. A loss of innocence, in a way.

It was both good and bad, and it was a sign of maturity.

Inside the kitchen, he stopped and watched her assess her surroundings. Her gaze narrowed on the calendar on the wall. It said May, a relief. From where he stood he couldn't see the year. He could only hope they'd arrived on time. "Storey."

When she didn't respond, he repeated it, "Storey."

"What?" She spun around when he didn't answer right away.

"I need to put her down."

Her gaze widened. "Oh geez. I'm so sorry. Come on, let's go up."

By now he knew the way, but suspected she wanted to see what her room looked like this time. He didn't care. His muscles were screaming and fatigue had taken over. He needed rest, too. At this rate, Tammy would wake and they wouldn't be able to sleep themselves because they'd need to look after her. His back was killing him, but there was no way he'd let Storey know. He was a ranger. They had an image to uphold. So how come there'd been no mention of rescuing damsels and children in distress anywhere in their manual?

Oh wait, what manual?

Storey opened the door and stepped inside. And

stopped.

He groaned silently. Now what?

"SO?" ERIC'S STRESSED voice prodded her forward.

"It looks the same." *Thank God.* "I can't tell you how glad I am to see that."

"But?"

She turned back toward him, confused. "But what?"

"You haven't entered fully," he snapped. "If everything is all right, let me in."

Finally, the impatience, fatigue and frustration in his voice hit her. She stepped aside quickly. He had to be exhausted. "Sorry, I'm tired too."

"And that's going to have to be something we address immediately." At the bed he leaned over to lay Tammy down. Storey rushed over. "Hang on." She pulled the covers back. "Now, lay her down. Maybe we'll be lucky and she'll sleep long enough for us to rest as well."

"I doubt it, but I need to crash regardless. I think the time travel stuff finished my system." Straightening, his gaze fell to the open floor. "I'm going to lie on the floor with that blanket if you don't mind?" He pointed at the one half falling off the end of her bed. Storey snatched it up and held it out to him.

"I'm thinking to lie down beside Tammy, actually."

Eric didn't even look at where she pointed. He'd stretched out on the floor, pulling her blanket over him. "Go ahead. I won't sleep long. A couple of hours should recharge me."

"Good for you. I doubt that little bit will do me," she muttered. Storey locked her bedroom door, turned out the light and curled up behind Tammy. The rodent opened his eyes, glared at her, realized she wasn't moving and returned to his spot in the crook of Tammy's arms.

She was so tired. Yet the thought of another Storey walking in on them was enough to keep her mind buzzing. She needed rest. She needed solutions. She'd needed this to all go back to normal.

Somehow.

While her mind pondered and fussed, Eric slept deeply on the floor beside her. His snores wafted gently through the room, making her smile. Then she was jealous. He could rest so easily. As if there weren't a million problems pressing in on them. She desperately needed rest, too. And a shower and a change of clothes and…she fell asleep.

"STOREY." HER SHOULDER was jostled. She frowned and tried to burrow deeper into her pillow.

The insistent voice wouldn't let up. "Storey, wake up."

She grumbled, "Too tired."

"I know you're tired, but there's a problem."

Storey's eyes slowly opened as that information filtered in. They were safe. They were home. So what was the big deal? Her mind flooded with memories. She sat up slowly, hating the screaming going on in her head, and felt tempted to ignore everything and go back to sleep. Her brain screamed for more sleep. "Eric? How long did we sleep?"

"I don't know. A couple of hours, maybe."

A dull daylight shone through the window. She stared out the window. The sky had turned black and clouds had gathered. "I think time travel must be harder on us than normal portal travel. I still feel like I have lead inside my bones." She yawned. "I just hope we're in the right time frame."

"Yes." His voice was grim. "But we have a bigger problem."

"What's the matter?" She studied his face.

"Tammy's missing."

She blinked. Once. Twice. Then panic hit. "Oh my God. Are you serious? I locked the door. I know I did."

"And she unlocked it."

Storey made it to her feet, swaying only slightly. She looked around and pointed out signs of Tammy's activities. A block of cheese sat on the desk, a large chunk ripped off, and an open package of pepperoni was almost gone. "She's found food at least."

Eric stared hungrily at the items. Storey rolled her eyes. "Grab it then. I'm going to go outside and see if she's there."

She stood up, searching for Tammy. "How long has she been gone?"

"I only woke up a few minutes ago. So I can't say."

"We have to find her," she said urgently. She stumbled to the door.

"I know." He said, explaining patiently. "That's why I came and woke you."

She checked her mother's bedroom. Empty. Downstairs, she checked out the various rooms and couldn't see any sign of Tammy. Out on the front deck, she searched the front of the house. Thankfully it appeared her parents hadn't returned. At least there were no vehicles at home.

At the outside chairs she found a stub of pepperoni. "At least we know she came this way."

Eric walked up behind her. "Great. So where'd she go from here?"

"I wish I knew how long she'd been gone. That would give me an idea of how far she could have traveled." Storey glanced out into the dark cloudy skies and ran her fingers through her hair. "I feel like I haven't slept in days."

"We haven't really. Portal travel, stress and even panic as we run for our lives, none of that is exactly easy on us, you know."

"I hear you." And she really didn't want to hear the details right now. Hadn't he mentioned brain damage in an earlier conversation? Nasty. She so didn't want to go there right now. She turned back to the real issue. "I really wish Tammy hadn't gone missing. I so don't need this."

"Actually…I'm not sure she has." He placed his hands on her shoulders and turned her gently. "Is that her? It looks almost like she's swinging on something like a suspended tire?"

Sure enough Tammy sat facing the other way on an old tire swing at the back of the neighbor's property. "Well thank heavens for that. One thing solved. Let's bring her back."

She started walking forward, Eric at her side, a chunk of cheese in one of his hands and a stick of pepperoni in the other. "You really love protein, don't you?"

"Protein?" He looked at the food in his hands.

"Meat. You could have grabbed an apple you know. Round out your food choices a little."

He grinned taking a big bite of cheese. "I'm good."

Males. She called out, "Tammy?"

Tammy spun around, saw them and a big grin lit her face. She opened her mouth and for the first time, a normal, or almost normal sounding voice came out. "Toey."

Storey grinned. "Almost. It's Storey with an Ssss sound."

Tammy tried again, her round face wrinkling with concentration. "Storrey."

"Close enough." Storey held out her hand. "Come on kiddo, back to the house."

Tammy hopped off, whistled sharply – at least her lips pursed the right motion, but it sounded more like air rushed out instead. But didn't the dratted rodent come running. He looked livelier too. He was dragging his leash behind. Tammy bent and grabbed the leash in one hand and her pet in the other.

The rest had done them all good. Storey had to admit she'd prefer to rest here for a day or two. Just sleep, shower, eat and repeat.

"I'm going to turn on the computer and check the dates."

"Will that tell you for sure?"

She frowned. "I can check the news and see what's happening. Computers are very exact nowadays."

"Hmmm."

"What are you thinking?" she asked curiously.

He glanced her and then away quickly. "I'm wondering about going back into time before the Louers crossed to their new dimension and make sure she's there for that crossing."

Storey's steps slowed as she considered the idea. "What would happen if we did something like that? Would we be messing with their future?"

"With Tammy's future maybe, in that she wouldn't remember any of this as it wouldn't have happened yet – in theory at least. If we returned in time to a point before Skorky ran away…and somehow stopped her from leaving the group…then she wouldn't have been there for you to find when you did."

"And I would have woken up still with my stylus and backpack and made a quick exit home. None of these last days would have happened." Her voice rose in excitement.

"In theory."

"And…would we remember it all? Or would we just not have those memories because we wouldn't have had these days?"

Eric shook his head. "I have no idea."

"It's a scary thought. It might be the best way to deal with Tammy's situation but is that the way to deal with anything else?"

"I don't think we can use it for much else though, at least not without messing with a lot of stuff."

It was her turn to say "Hmmm, I suppose." But her mind wouldn't let go of the concept. If it would return her world to normal that would be huge. But how could she do that without messing up the Louers' dimension?

Back at the house, Storey took everyone back to her room and turned on her laptop. It sat under a pile of clothes. She'd forgotten about it in their last few crazy trips. Once up, with Eric and Tammy crowding around, both of them eating apples this time, Storey checked the date. May 17th. Close enough. Checking out the news, as far as she could see, they were back where they belonged.

"Thank heavens for that," she murmured, relief slipping off her shoulders.

He wrapped one arm around her shoulder and squeezed. She smiled. Behind her, a telephone rang. She turned, a frown forming. Should she answer it or not?

"Aren't you going to answer it?" He dropped his arm and took a step back.

"It won't be for me. I have a cell phone."

But her feet walked in that direction. Slowly, she picked it up. "Hello."

"Storey? Where the hell have you been?"

Storey didn't recognize the irate voice. "Who is this?"

"Your father, of course. Who do you think?" Sarcasm dripped through the phone line. "Where have you been?"

"Um, doing homework?" she wrinkled her face at Eric, whispering the identity of the caller. He frowned at her.

She shrugged and spoke into the phone. "When are you coming home?"

"I'll be there in three hours, maybe four. I want you there when I get back, do you hear me? You mother and I have been worried sick. There's been a mess of weird storms going on, communications have been down all over the place. I know our phone hasn't been working but that's no reason for making us worry."

Storey didn't know what to say. Thankfully she didn't appear to need to say anything as his irate voice rolled right over her. "Stay home. We'll get there as soon as we're done working. I'm going to phone your mother right now and let her know you're okay."

Storey made what she thought might have been the appropriate response as he hung up a few seconds later. She shook her head. "What the heck. He said they've been having weird storms, communications down? That's not because of us, is it?"

Eric waved as if to brush off the idea, then paused, his hand in the air. His face twisted with concentration. "I'd have said no, until I remembered the time travel." He stood with his hands on his hips contemplating the flooring. "With that, it is very possible. Think about it. We can't just move through time-space without a reaction of some kind. Energy has to shift and change, atmospheres have to adapt, the time–space continuum has an order and we've disturbed it." He shrugged as if expecting her to understand all that he'd spouted off. "Weather anomalies could easily be experienced with those changes."

She winced. "Great. So we're screwing with the weather patterns, too. Is nothing going our way?" she muttered the last bit under her breath, but Eric still heard her.

"We're doing fine. We're back to the time period we belong in, now the stylus can help us to get Tammy home."

She brightened. "Let's ask. My parents are going to be home in three hours, four maximum. Possibly earlier. We need to be gone, and hopefully back again before they get home."

Eric motioned toward the bedroom where Tammy stood in the doorway a worried look on her face. Storey rushed forward, a reassuring smile on her face. "It's okay honey. Everything is fine." At least her tone of voice had to help even if Tammy didn't understand the words.

Coming up behind both of them, Eric ushered them into the bedroom, closing and locking the door behind them. "Let's get this done."

Storey pulled out her largest sketchbook from the closet. Seeing an older backpack stuffed in the back, she grabbed it too. Then she sat cross-legged with her stylus. "Stylus, we need to get Tammy back to her family. Not just any Louers but to her mother and father. How do we do that?"

The stylus jerked in her hand, Storey slapped the tip on the paper. She read the answer out to Eric. "Going back in time is dangerous. Going to her family in their new dimension right now is also dangerous."

Eric shook his head. "Staying here isn't an option.

Tammy needs her family and because of you, she trusts us to take her home."

"Which option do you want to choose?" She studied Eric's face looking for an answer.

"Which is the least dangerous?" Eric countered.

Going to her family now. You won't have to factor in all the dimension shifts from a time change.

"Fine. Let's do that then. Give us the coordinates for her people, preferably her parents, so that we can land, give her to them, and get out again. This time in and out. No landing us in weird spots or other time frames. Clean and simple."

Storey took note of the determination in his jaw as he spoke. She wished it could be so easy.

The humming filled the air, this time louder, more intense as if the stylus was trying to actually transport them there himself. Storey looked over at Eric, one eyebrow raised. He shrugged. They both waited.

Tammy sidled closer, slipping her hand into Storey's hand. The two girls leaned against each other as they waited. She figured the stylus had to be communicating with the other styluses. Or it was recharging. Shrugging it off, she concentrated on the problems at hand. Time was running out.

"We'll need to change clothes," she said abruptly.

"Why? I haven't."

"You can't," she said wryly. "There aren't any other clothes here that will fit you."

An odd light flashed in his eyes and it matched the grin flashing across his face. Standing, he pulled a flat object out of a weird side pocket just below his knee of his ranger pants. "I forgot. They missed this when they emptied my pockets. Not that they'd have known its value anyway." At her frown, he laughed. "Exactly. You have no idea what this is, do you?"

She studied it for a moment. As it was too small to be anything but a plastic business card or credit card, she couldn't see any other purpose to it. Especially being as thin as it was. "Nope."

With a huge grin, he said, "Watch, you're gonna love this." He pulled a clip off the outside of his pants pocket. It was the size of a small cell phone. She'd thought it had been a decoration. Typical. He connected the clip to his small envelope looking thing, then tapped the small flat surface several times. Musical notes sounded, almost in a melody she recognized. Even Tammy came rushing over at the tune.

Then Eric held the small package slightly away from his body. The package, apparently unlocked by the music, swelled and reshaped into a large rectangle as if folded under pressure. By the time it stopped moving, the package was now several feet long and a good foot wide.

The process had taken less than a minute.

Her astonishment made him laugh. "If you tell me that there is a full change of clothes in there, I'm so going to get me one of those."

Eric laughed as he opened the package to pull out pants, a shirt and what looked like socks. "I've got several spares on me all the time."

She gasped. "And you didn't offer me the same thing?"

He said apologetically, "I never considered it. I wondered why you were putting all that stuff into your bag. But it's your dimension, your house, your system. I've been trying to learn how you do things here."

"I did that because I didn't have another choice," she snapped, exasperated. She stopped, a cool idea coming into her mind. "Does that only work with material?"

He frowned, not understanding.

"Could you do that to my sketchbooks, papers, food, anything?

"Everyone in my dimension carries things this way. And yes, we could carry blankets, clothing, sketchbooks. I don't know about food as I've never tried."

Storey bent and upended her bag of collected goodies. The mess rolled everywhere. "Go for it."

Eric gave her a shuttered look but bent obediently and separated the items into perishable and nonperishable. The nonperishable items he converted to a small bagful almost immediately. Once he had things sorted, he took the same cell phone thingy, clipped it to a corner of the bag, tapped several different spots, producing a different musical tune and the magic happened in reverse. While Storey watched in amazement, a long brown film stretched over the end of the stack and within seconds it had compressed and shrunken to a small envelope size.

Eric stood and held it out to her.

She studied it, turning it over and over, all the while shaking her head. "Wow. I don't know how much you can put into a package like this but my world needs this technology."

"It's tied to our codex technology. This way people can carry what they need to travel."

"Right." Her frown deepened. "So we can't have it. How can I open it without that little musical thingy? What's it called anyway?" She couldn't believe how fascinating and practical this system was. She so wanted one of those tools.

"It's a codin." He laughed lightly. "We all have them. Several in some cases."

"Is there a way to open it if we get separated?"

His grin flashed again. "I suspect the stylus would be

able to open it for you if I'm not around."

"Except I need the sketchbook in here to communicate," she said in exasperation.

"Not quite. You seem to do fine even without paper. I wonder if there's a way for you to become telepathic with it?"

"Yes. I just don't know how yet." Unfortunately. "Can you do another of those little packages up? To hold spares of everything and another for food?"

Eric pulled another clip from his knee pocket and attached it to his codin.

Boy did she want to have that technology for herself. "Do you know how much easier it would be to travel if I could do that with all my stuff?"

"It has limits, but for the most part, it's a wonderful convenience."

She snorted. "Ya think? What's the limit for this type of thing?"

Eric assessed the food stacked in front of him. "I've only used it for packing clothing and personal items." He grinned sheepishly. "That spare has been in these pants for awhile now. We could have done this so much earlier, but honestly, your system worked so well, I never considered looking for an alternative."

What could she say to that? Nothing. With time marching against them, she quickly drew a portal to Paxton's lab while Eric packed clothing and food in separate parcels in case they were separated or captured again. In the packets Storey included two portals that they could use. The one they'd use to bring them home and the one to Paxton's lab.

Now, prepared with these, Storey had to admit the concept of going back with Tammy wasn't so daunting.

The deck was stacked in her favor for once.

CHAPTER 14

"ARE YOU SURE you want to leave before your parents get home?" Eric waited for her answer patiently.

She'd been warring with herself for the last ten minutes over that same issue. "Yeah. I can't even begin to explain you three being here." As much as she'd like to smooth things over and leave on a good note, how could she without bringing up more problems? She didn't even know this man who called himself her father. He might use the same name…but that didn't make him the same man. Which he obviously wasn't as he'd stuck around in this reality.

Making a sudden decision, she walked over to her desk and wrote a note on the pad of paper sitting there, reading it out as she wrote. "Sorry. I have to leave. I'll be back in a couple of hours."

Staring at the message for a long moment, she decided it would have to do. Hopefully she'd be back in time to ditch the note before they ever saw it.

She marched back over to where Tammy, holding Skorky tucked firmly under her arm with her hand in Eric's, waited for her. At Eric's questioning look, she shrugged. "I don't know what else to do."

His lopsided grin flashed. "It's pretty messed up, isn't it?"

"Ya think," she sniffed. "Do we know what we're doing

this time? Do we need to meet with Paxton? Get another codex?" Eric frowned, considering. "It would be a good idea. If nothing else we should report in."

Storey glanced at Tammy. Paxton wouldn't be happy if she returned with them. "Before or after?"

He grimaced as he understood her meaning. "Before would be better, but afterward would be easier on Paxton."

"We can't forget the missing portals and codexes. A second team to retrieve those would be easier on us."

This time excitement lit Eric's face. "Now that would be awesome."

"I know." Still she felt a cautionary note was needed. "Do you have any idea what happened to your father?" She frowned and walked over to the pad of paper on her desk. "Stylus, please send a message to Paxton letting him know where we are and the problem we had of the time dimensional issue."

"He knows," she read out loud. "I've kept him informed." She shook her head. "Oh. Good, I guess. So he knows we're at my house with Tammy still?"

No. Telling him now.

Storey waited. "Could you also ask if Eric's father has been located?"

No sign of him yet.

Storey and Eric exchanged worried looks. "I don't know if I should be worried for you or happy for me," she said in a wry voice. "I don't want anything bad to happen to him, I just want to have him be nice to me. Or better yet, have nothing to do with me."

Eric bent his head to the paper, as if waiting for another immediate communication. "I know. I don't like this though. It's been days. There's no place he could go."

"Could he go to another dimension?"

"He'd be scared to come here, and the Louers, well, he was in a panic the one time I helped him and the others escape from there. I can't see him willingly going back."

"So where could he be?" Storey shook her head. "I'm an idiot. Stylus, where is the Councilman?"

She rolled her eyes at Eric. "How could we not have asked it?"

Humming filled the air. It fascinated her as the stylus had no source of power or speakers. "How can it make that noise?"

"Just another of the wonders of the stylus."

The humming stopped and Storey's hand jerked as it started writing. She closed her eyes, almost seeing the message in her mind. With a little practice she could probably get the message without needing paper. But to create portals she'd still need paper – at least she thought so. At the rate her skills and knowledge had developed, who knew?

The Councilman is not in Eric's dimension.

"Oh shit."

She stared at Eric in shock. "Stylus, which dimension is he in?"

The new Louer home.

Eric reached out a hand and gripped Storey's shoulder. "What? Is that really possible?"

"Stylus? How did the Councilman get over there?"

He was taken as a prisoner.

Storey closed her eyes. Her stomach sank. This conversation was not going to be good. "What? How?"

He contacted the Louers to have them take care of you. You escaped, so they snatched him instead.

Swallowing painfully at the hard truths, Storey asked, "Stylus, please relay this information to Paxton."

Eric stumbled back several feet to the window. Storey knew if the truth had hurt her, it had to have devastated him.

"Which group of Louers took him as prisoner? And how did he contact the Louers?"

The ones that grabbed Tammy. Paxton entered the new coordinates from Eric's codex into the database. The Councilman used those to program his codex.

Storey sighed and stared at Eric. So much for a quick in and out trip. "How could he possibly communicate with them?" Storey wondered aloud. "Then again, we didn't try to talk to them very much, did we? We judged their communication abilities based on Tammy."

Most Louers have baseline English. An older version than you would know, but still understandable. Between themselves they use telepathy.

The stylus started moving faster. *Storey, this is Paxton. It's imperative that you rescue the Councilman from those people.*

It was on the tip of Storey's tongue to ask why when the asshole had contacted the Louers to take her out. She couldn't come up with one good reason why she should. From the fury on Eric's face, neither could he. "Stylus, is the Councilman in the same caves where we found Tammy?"

Yes.

"Oh shit." Storey looked at Eric. "Tammy needs to go home. She can't get involved in this. You know the Louers would love to recapture her. We can't take that chance."

Paxton sent another message. *This is a crisis for our people. Eric must come and plan the Councilman's return.*

"Eric, what do you want to do?"

"Leave my father to the fate he created." Eric's glower had Tammy creeping behind Storey, her hand slipping into Storey's pocket.

Storey patted her on the shoulder.

"That's what I *want* to do, but I don't know what we *should* do." Eric stared off into the night, the anger fading slightly from his eyes as he considered the problem a little longer.

Storey couldn't see an immediate solution either. She really didn't want to rescue someone who had tried to get rid of her. She valued her life. Why would she save his so he could try and take hers – again?

Still this was Eric's call.

Eric nodded. "We should leave him there. It would serve him right."

"And would that serve your people's needs, as well?" she asked curiously. There was much she didn't understand about the way his world worked, his government processes or even the way someone came into power. "Was your father born into his leadership position?"

Eric spun around. From the look on his face, she'd take that as a no. "Of course not. He was elected to the Council and then voted to the head."

"So he can be voted off? Removed from his position because of bad behavior?" She watched the change of emotions ripple across his features.

Eric hitched his hands on his hips, his head cocked to one side. "It's possible, but I've yet to see it happen."

"No one has ever been voted out?" Her astonishment sharpened her voice. Were they nuts? "How long has he been in power?"

"He's been the Councilman all my life. I've never known

a time when he wasn't."

Something was wrong with that system. The Councilman was an unbalanced individual who'd allowed his own feelings to direct his actions. Actions that didn't make him look good. Maybe he'd been a good man, a strong leader...before Storey had jumped into his life. She had to believe he'd served his people well at one time.

It's not as if her society didn't have prejudices themselves. To Eric's father she was an offworlder. An alien, almost.

"I want to leave him where he is for a while," he snapped. "But I can't. And that makes me mad. He should stay there. After the despicable things he's done, he deserves to suffer."

She could so understand. But like him, she knew it wasn't the right thing to do. "What's the chance he's learned his lesson?"

"Not him." Eric shook his head violently. "He's very powerful here. Believes he can do anything."

"Because you've all allowed him to think that way. He's been like a king over you all."

Eric shot her a disgusted look. "I know. But it's not going to be that way anymore."

"Not if you leave him there." She grinned. "You could make it a condition of helping him return."

He studied her before grudgingly nodding. "Not bad. I could slip home and talk to them, maybe organize a back up team to help us, then come back here."

Storey hated to see him go. He might never come back. But a second team would be a wonderful idea. "Go. At least to meet with your Council and determine what's to be done. I don't want you to go at all." She gave him a lopsided grin.

"But it's something that you need to do."

He tilted his head and narrowed his gaze. "Yes, I do, but I want you to come to me in an hour. That way I won't have to worry about missing my meeting with you or worry about you going over there without me. I'll tell Paxton you three are due to join us in one hour. Don't be late," he warned. "Your arrival will be the necessary impetus to get them to talk. To actually make a decision about what to do."

"I'll need a portal to Paxton's lab though, please."

Rolling her eyes, she quickly sketched out a new one, then dropped it on her floor. She took a step back.

"Remember, one hour."

Tammy clung to Storey's hand. Storey confirmed, "We'll be there."

He gave them a long look, then stepped through and disappeared.

Just like that, they were alone.

ERIC HATED LEAVING Storey. Pressure squeezed his chest tight. It wasn't so much the separation, although that was part of it, but more the fact that everything was screwing up – no matter what they did. He didn't know if it was the stylus, the damage to the dimensions, or something worse. With everything so unstable, he hated leaving her behind. And Tammy.

The black mist dissipated. Eric looked around, frowning. Paxton's lab was deserted. Not all that unusual, but given the unpredictable events that had recently occurred, it didn't make him feel any better. Striding to the conference room, he found Paxton and the Council members in session.

Paxton broke off speaking, relief washing over his face as

he caught sight of Eric. Standing, he cried, "There you are." A worried look slipped onto his face as he peered around behind Eric, "Are you alone?"

Eric glanced over his shoulder, only realizing as he did so that Paxton was asking about Storey…and maybe about Tammy as well. "Yes," he said brusquely. As Paxton sat back again, relaxed and happy, he added, "but not for long. Both Storey and Tammy will be here in less than an hour."

He'd have laughed if he could have at the look of horror on his mentor's face. "You called me back here, remember. We were having some big issues over there."

Paxton's white wispy hair bobbed as he nodded. "I understand that. But they can't come here. You'll have to stop them."

"No. I'm not going to. I'm not sending Storey and Tammy back to the Louer world alone. That's just foolish. We tried once and that ended in disaster."

The Council had listened with rapt attention to this point but no more. First one then another piped up with questions.

"Who is Tammy?"

"What disaster?"

Paxton glared at him. Eric shrugged. "Maybe they should know. The girls will be here soon. Besides, you brought me home."

"Know what?" Council member Eragin spoke up. Middle-aged and portly he had a self-professed air of importance like the other Council members, but he'd always been straightforward in his dealings with Eric.

Eric raised a brow in question to Paxton. Paxton held a unique position here. He had more seniority than many of the members added together and he headed the science and technology institute, but essentially he lived in the lab. He'd also been Eric's mentor and dare he say – friend – for most of Eric's life. He was a much bigger influence in Eric's life than his own father. That had to be a good thing, considering the mess his father was currently stirring up.

Paxton sighed, ran his fingers through his hair, then nodded. "Let's have everything out in the open."

"Good." The telling took a bit, but Eric finally brought the members up to speed on where he and Storey had been and the problems they'd encountered in the process. With another look at Paxton, he asked, "How much do they know of my father's situation?"

He was almost sorry for asking. Paxton aged in front of him, his wrinkles deepened and the look in his eyes…well, for that alone, Eric was sorry he'd mentioned the subject. Paxton's eyes flattened to black and the sadness Eric saw there would have made him weep on any other day.

"I'm sorry," he said gently, hating that his father could do this to such a good man. "If we're going to stop this vicious cycle we have to get things out in the open and keep them there."

"I know." Paxton cleared his throat. "I'll explain this part."

That was good. It not only allowed Eric some assimilation time, it also allowed him a chance to observe the reactions of the six council members. Their expressions ranged from horror to fear and one older fellow, Marxel, just didn't get it. Even after several explanations he still didn't seem to understand what the Councilman had done.

By the time he did, they'd wasted precious minutes. Eric couldn't resist checking the time for the umpteenth time. Now Storey would be there in a half hour. "The meeting needs to get on track. The girls will be here very soon." He waited a moment and then said into the silence, "What do you want to do about my father?"

There. It was out in the open. His father had made some bad decisions and someone needed to make an official decision. This was personal for Eric. He didn't really want his father left over there, no matter how tempting an idea initially.

"I do however have several stipulations to put forth. If I go to rescue my father, I won't see him return to his position of power. He abused his station and he's tried to hurt someone who has only been a friend to us. Should your decision be that the Councilman will regain his title once he has been rescued, then—"

"No, the Councilman has lost his title. I confronted your father. He admitted to changing Storey's codex to send her to the Louers' dimension. Based on that the council held an emergency meeting and told him he was done. He disappeared shortly after that." Paxton ran a hand through his wispy hair. "I suspect he's done this to extract revenge on the person he blames for everything that has gone wrong in his life."

Eric settled back on his heels. That actually made sense.

"We need to vote on his replacement – something that hasn't had to be done in decades. So while he still holds the title, it and he are now powerless."

Eric gave a short nod. "Good. So plans?"

The discussion became hot and heavy as suggestions were offered and rejected as the top brains and strategists of Eric's city put their heads together. He listened carefully, happy when his lowly opinion was asked for and his suggestions listened to. During the meeting several of his supervisors came and went as potential actions were considered by everyone.

There was no consensus. The various suggestions were problematic. Eric knew that to cross over with large numbers as a show of force could cause problems with the dimensional energy again. It was also liable to destroy the Louers and only a small portion of those people were responsible for either of the kidnappings. As with every civilization, there were small renegade groups that gave the other people a bad name. His father had just become an example in his own society.

"Stealth is required," he said, his voice firm. "A small force. In and out. Using our codexes, we should be able to travel close to the group, rescue the Councilman and slip home before the Louers know what's happened. If we go in with a large force, we are asking for trouble and…" he paused, thinking about how he and Storey had woken up after somehow being knocked out, "they may have a weapon or skill we can't compete with."

At their outraged looks he filled them in on what had happened.

Paxton interrupted, "Are you sure they didn't knock you out?"

Of everyone, he seemed the most upset. Eric wasn't sure if it was because of the treatment he'd received or the fact that the Louers might have superior technology. True, his people had amazing technology, but they'd achieved it through industrial espionage. If Storey's people had the same technology he had no doubt they'd have developed it much further than his people.

"No, I was not knocked out physically. It might be a telepathic weapon, since they communicate this way most of the time."

That set them off again. Eric sat back and tried to let it wash over him, their voices like the cacophony of a rising hurricane.

As in the eye of the storm, silence descended.

Then horrified gasps sounded.

The eye lasted barely a few seconds, then the storm hit.

Eric opened his eyes to find the council standing and almost shouting as a group, their arms pointing at the doorway. Eric turned.

Storey. And Tammy. And Skorky.

CHAPTER 15

S TOREY LOOKED OVER at him and rolled her eyes. Eric gave a shout of laughter and went to stand behind them, an arm on the shoulders of each girl. He waited for the men to calm down. For Marxel, it seemed as if the shock was almost too much. He sat, a gray cast to his skin, and seemed barely able to open his mouth. Eric motioned at Paxton, who immediately rushed to his old friend.

"I'm fine. Or I will be when I get rid of this abomination."

Storey's back stiffened. How dare he? Tammy clung closer, almost crawling up Storey's legs. She frowned at the elder. "Would that be me, Tammy or Skorky that you are calling an abomination?"

Eric squeezed her shoulder. "Easy," he whispered.

The elder's mouth opened and closed several times but no words came out. Storey nodded once and released her gaze on the hapless man to stare at Paxton.

Paxton rushed to speak. "Now, Storey, remember to see a Louer here in the chambers, particularly after the recent problem, is going to cause some distress."

"Of course," she said coolly. "As long as everyone is aware she is a child and a victim here. Not an aggressive warrior. She deserves our help. Not our hate."

The rumble of dissent had her sticking her jaw out.

Speaking loudly to get over the din, she said, "You called Eric home when we were going to make another attempt to return this child to her family. If we can rescue the Councilman, something I'm not terribly in favor of given his behavior toward me, then I'm game to lend a hand. Otherwise, my priority at the moment is getting Tammy home."

All eyes focused on Tammy.

"She's a juvenile Louer?" One of the men at the back of the room spoke up. With so many staring at her, Storey didn't know which one.

"Yes. The animal is her pet." Taking advantage of the calmer atmosphere, she quickly gave an explanation as to how she and Tammy had met.

Understanding lit some of their faces, others showed no softening.

"How can we use this?"

Again, Storey couldn't see the speaker. "The group that grabbed Tammy is the same group that is holding the Councilman. She can't be taken back there. Her life is in danger."

"We should trade her. We'd get rid of two problems at once."

Storey gasped, unwittingly squeezing Tammy's hand. Tammy opened her mouth and the noise that screamed out of her mouth had everyone in the room clapping their hands over their ears and crying out. Storey slipped off her backpack and with Eric's help dug in to find a granola bar. Pulling it out, Storey held it out for Tammy who snatched it up with teary eyes. The noise shut off immediately.

"Good God, what was that?"

"That was the scream of betrayal for an adult who'd trade a defenseless child for a lying, cheating, vindictive

Councilman," she snapped, her fury so great she doubted she'd be able to control what came out of her mouth if anyone said anything else about throwing Tammy to her death.

The room full of men stilled.

Behind her, Eric whispered, "I think that's the first time they've ever been told off."

"It's too bad," she bit off, "that this attitude is allowed to permeate through your people. It doesn't show any of you in a good light."

Knowing the others heard her, she added, "Reminds me of the actions of the same person you're asking us to go save." Her smile, grim and ferocious, beamed as she added, "That was also a death sentence."

Silence. The elders looked at each other, then down at their various papers. Paxton didn't appear to know how to answer that.

Eric spoke up, his tone placating, as if hoping to soothe the storm. "Time is an issue here. They were prepared to sacrifice Tammy within days. My father could face the same fate."

Paxton bolted to his feet. "You must go. Return Tammy then travel to where the Councilman is being held. While you gain intelligence, we'll pull a party together to meet you there. Time it to the minute. The team will port in, rescue him and all can return home. With enough codexes, the trip will take only minutes."

The rest of the elders sighed happily. Obviously, with a proactive plan finally put forward, they were prepared to jump behind it.

"Good. You do that." Storey turned abruptly and tugged Tammy back into the other room. Tammy followed obediently, still munching on her treat. Skorky sat in her hood, delicately working on his piece of bar.

"Hey wait, what's the matter?" Eric called out behind her, racing to catch up.

"Nothing," she said. At least nothing more than all of the things wrong in her world right now. "We're so far behind schedule. If we stay here and do nothing but let them rant, Tammy will be our age before they get the plan moving. This way, we can take care of one problem, while they work on another problem."

She spun around, wondering at his silence. "Right?"

"Right." He grinned. "I'm just thinking we should have you attend all the Council meetings to get things done."

She shot him a horrified look. "Do you hate me that much?"

His grin flashed wickedly. "No, I like you that much I'd like to find reasons to keep you closer."

"Oh," she brightened. "For that reason alone, I'd consider it, but I can tell you right now that those old farts in there wouldn't let it happen."

He wrapped an arm around her shoulders and chucked the ever silent Tammy under the chin making her laugh. "I'm up for anything that keeps you in my world."

"Are you talking to Tammy or me?" At his look, she snickered. "Come on, let's return Tammy to her family, although I'm going to miss her something awful. And to think we're going to rescue your father now."

"He might learn something from this adventure." He laughed and tugged her toward the corner of the lab where the portal was.

"Yeah," she said darkly, "he might be worse now!"

Before she knew it the black smoke had risen to her

waist. Tammy snuggled in close.

"I wish she could talk."

In the back of her head, a small voice said, "I do talk. Why can't you hear me?"

Storey shot a startled look at Tammy. Then blackness took over and she couldn't see or hear anything.

ERIC JUST BARELY caught an odd look on Storey's face before everything went dark. He tightened his arm around her shoulder, reassured as she cuddled closer. Tammy's arms wrapped tight around both of them. He had to admit, it wasn't going to be easy to say good-bye to her. Not being able to speak had kept them from learning anything about her people or lifestyle, but had maybe made the visit a little easier on them if her speech and communication abilities were anything like her screaming.

That noise she made had to be a lethal weapon.

The black fog started to recede.

The trip seemed longer this time. They'd had so many problems traveling lately that he no longer had the same assurance that all would be well. Still, if one didn't understand all the things that could go wrong, then it was impossible to be prepared.

Maybe that was a good thing.

He studied the familiar looking trees. "Looks like we're here."

"Hmm. Wherever here is?" Storey stepped back and checked out the sky and the surrounding hilly terrain. "It looks different than the last location."

Eric checked out the trees that dotted the landscape. "It's similar – we could be close to the last spot – but I don't recognize the area.”

“Let’s head over there.” Storey pointed to the grove of evergreen trees in the distance.

“Why trees again?”

“I don’t know. I guess I’d feel better if we weren’t out in the open like this…”

“Got it.” He was good with that. “First things first. Give me your codex.” He unclipped both of them, and a quick glance toward Tammy, he dropped them into a different pocket on his left leg. With Tammy busy looking around, she never even saw the movement. He gave a soft chuckle, then led the way, trying to keep an eye on the open fields around them.

The closer they got to the trees however, the more nervous Storey started to act. She turned to look behind them several times, even to the point of turning around and walking backwards to check out the area.

“What’s the matter?”

“I don’t know,” she admitted. “It’s like a weird buzzing in my head. Sometimes at my home, when I walk beside a large hydro station, I can hear a similar sound. I almost recognize it, but it shouldn’t exist in this location.”

“Hydro station?”

She shook her head. “Creates electricity for our cities.”

“Electricity?”

“Yeah, you know lights to see by, stoves to cook with, monitors to keep an eye on crossings; they all plug into wall outlets that provide the necessary power to make them run.” She walked a few moments in silence then sighed. “You don’t have that kind of power, do you?”

He shook his head. “Not like that. We have fuel cells that keep things running. But I think our requirements are much less than yours."

They'd almost reached the grove of trees, when Tammy started. She tugged on Storey's arm until Storey looked at her. "What's the matter?"

Tammy pointed.

Storey spun around but Eric was way ahead of her.

"Louers."

STOREY STIFFENED. MEETING the Louers was why they were here, but after their last meeting, she didn't trust them. The buzz in the air deepened. She studied Tammy's face looking for some sign that she might recognize the approaching Louers. Her face appeared normal. Not fearful, not worried, and yet, not happy. Very frustrating.

Eric whispered, "Careful."

That's when Storey realized she'd been retreating steadily. "Sorry." She glanced at him. "What is that noise? It's getting worse."

He frowned. "I don't hear it.

"Tammy appears unaffected."

Eric bent around Storey to check out Tammy's face. "So does that mean she knows them or doesn't know them? It's so frustrating she can't speak. We know she has healthy vocal cords and lungs."

Storey studied the approaching group. None were familiar. The buzz in her head deepened. She had to consider the idea that had trickled into her consciousness earlier. "I think the buzz is her people using telepathic communication. I heard it last time too."

He gripped her shoulders then relaxed slightly. "I can barely hear it."

The newcomers kept walking toward them. "They probably used a form of the same ability to knock us unconscious, too."

Eric walked several steps to the side to study Tammy's face. "She's busy doing something. If it isn't communicating with the approaching group then I don't know what else it could be."

"When we were in the portal, I thought Tammy spoke to me in my head." Storey hoped it had been her. She'd love to be able to talk to her.

"If it was her," Eric suggested, "that could mean you are receptive to their method but need to have the distractions filtered out so you can hear her."

That made sense. Just the thought of being able to communicate with Tammy was exciting. "Is the energy thinner, different in the portal?"

He nodded. They'd come to a dead stop, waiting until the Louers walked closer. Keeping his voice low, he answered, "Yes. The portal blocks everything else out."

"If I could learn to communicate with her, then in theory, I could learn to communicate with my stylus. That would be perfect."

She kept her eye on the leader of the group, a large overbearing male who strode slightly ahead of another dozen in their group. At least he didn't have any numbers on his arms. "I'm not liking this."

"Who is?"

Storey alternated between studying the group and then Tammy's face. "I don't understand why they have no facial expressions. It's like they are emotionless."

"Until you look them in the eyes."

At his words, Storey shifted her gaze to study the leader's

eyes. Huge, deep set and dark, so dark it was hard to see if he had the same eye biology she had. She hadn't noticed any difference in Tammy's eyes.

His eyes weren't cold though; dark, curious, wary, yes. Certainly not emotionless. Interesting. She kept her hand resting on Tammy's shoulder – nonthreatening but protective. She didn't know what was about to happen but if anyone made a crosswise move against her…Storey planned to bolt – with Tammy. If she couldn't be assured of Tammy's safety, she wasn't leaving her behind.

Not that she had any idea of where to take her. *So please let everything work out.*

As the group approached, she watched all eyes zero in on Tammy. The buzzing in the air pumped up. Tammy started bouncing, her fingers were clenching Storey's hand so tightly, Storey didn't realize she was squeezing back so hard, Tammy couldn't go to see the others even if she wanted to.

Finding it difficult to do, Storey forced herself to let go of the little girl's hand. As if freed by an elastic band, Tammy shot forward and launched herself into the lead male's arms.

Eric and Storey inched closer, watching as Tammy was caught and held in a tight grip.

"Well, that's good news."

"It looks that way. We don't know that this is Tammy's father, but I guess it's safe to say that she's happy to see him."

"And he her." The group continued to march toward them, only now Tammy was wrapped tight in the leader's arms.

Her back straightened as the group stopped several feet in front of Storey. Storey didn't want to break eye contact with the leader but at the same time, she wanted to make sure Tammy was happy. Giving the little girl a quick look, she found her staring back at Storey. Storey couldn't help but smile at her.

For the first time, Tammy's lips curved upward in response.

"Tammy, that's perfect. I'm happy to see you smiling."

Tammy wiggled and the man holding her let her go. Tammy came running over to Storey and threw her arms tight around her waist. Storey bent and hugged her back. Skorky ran around Tammy's shoulders as if too excited to sit still. The others watched.

Tammy released Storey then hugged Eric in turn. He grinned at her. "I'm going to miss you, Tammy."

She ran back to the big male and stood at his side.

Then she turned to face them, waved at them both.

The world dimmed.

Storey watched as Eric crumpled to the ground in front of her.

"No." She struggled to stay on her feet.

The ground rushed to meet her.

CHAPTER 16

ERIC WINCED AT the sound. Someone was groaning, retching in a rhythm he recognized but didn't want to. The fumes of heavy stomach acid hit his nose just then and it was all he could do to not vomit himself. He had no idea who was sick, but he was about to join them if they didn't stop soon.

Then he heard a sound, just a faint moan, but it was enough. "Storey."

"Oh God, I hope not. That would mean I was here, caught in this no man's land still. Why couldn't it be like my clone or something?"

Eric laughed. Even feeling like crap, with her voice so woozy, her spunky attitude made him laugh. She might be sick but she wasn't screaming in pain and if her sense of humor was still there, things couldn't be that bad.

He opened his eyes. Where were they?

"Storey, are we prisoners again?"

"I have no idea. I can hardly move for the pain in my head."

Eric tried to sit up, and a hammer-sized boom exploded inside his head. Groaning, he collapsed back down. "What did they do to us?" he whispered when he could.

"I have no idea. We're in some kind of cave again. At least that's all I can see. There's no opening and it kind of reminds me of the Louers' old dimension except for one huge thing missing – the smell."

Eric sniffed the air experimentally. The last place he wanted to find himself was back in that horrible dimension, but if the Louers could do things like they'd done to Storey and him without them even letting on how they'd been done, he'd be happy to leave and never come back.

And he still had to rescue his father.

Gritting his teeth, he sat up very slowly and looked around. The air was murky. He could make out Storey but not much else.

"Wise of you to take it slow. I made the mistake of jumping up." Storey tried to smile, but gave up the attempt. "After that the contents of my stomach came rushing up, too."

"At least we're together."

"True." she agreed. "If you're awake enough, and my stomach has settled enough, can we port away from here? It looks like we're still prisoners and I'm really not wanting to be around when they come back."

Eager relief swept through him at her words. "Did they leave us a portal?"

"If we still have the packets, then I think so. I hope so."

Eric checked his ranger pants. Good. He still had the same packet that they'd missed last time. It should have a portal.

Storey found hers, too. "Looks like we're good. I'm surprised considering Tammy saw us pack up these. I don't know how much she understood of codexes and portals. I'm really hoping she didn't comprehend much."

Eric winced, realizing just how much an older Louer would have understood if they'd seen what Tammy had seen.

"Let's hope she's too young to give an accurate account."

"Yeah, you think?" Storey handed over her traveling packet. "Codex or portal?"

Within seconds he had it open. She grabbed the spare shirt from the package.

"Codex." He pulled two spares out of the pockets and held them up with a big grin. "They didn't take these."

"Yay!" Storey turned her back to him, quickly changing her shirt.

"Why are you changing?"

She snorted. "My shirt took a hit when my stomach emptied. I don't really want to be wearing my lunch for the rest of the day, thank you."

Turning back, she asked, "Eric, can you repackage all this?"

Eric looked up from his codex, frowning. "Yes. Have you got everything you need? We should have thrown your backpack in there."

"Practice makes perfect," she muttered. He was right, but she didn't need to be reminded of it. Fascinated, she watched the clothing and other items, minus her sketchbook, shrink into a tiny packet. She so needed that technology. Every female did, no matter what dimension they occupied.

"Are you ready?"

Storey looked over at him. Her travel pouch was safely stored away. "Yes."

Even as she spoke, she heard the sounds he'd obviously already heard.

Footsteps.

"Shit." She raced over to his side. "Let's go."

As she finished speaking, the black mist wrapped around her feet. Eric's arms came around her shoulders, tugging her close. "Say good-bye to Tammy."

"Oh." Storey leaned back. "I hope she's going to be okay now."

"She should be fine."

That's not quite what she wanted to hear, but as the mist rose, the choice to change things disappeared. They still had to find a way to fix the portal between the old and new Louer world. If such a thing were possible. Should she leave a note for Tammy's father, explaining the portal's new functionality? Maybe she'd get the chance to say good-bye then.

"She'll be fine," Eric whispered against her hair. "Tammy is with people that know her and we're going to believe that she's loved."

Storey knew he was right, but…even though she'd seen Tammy held high and happy in the leader's arms, she felt like she'd deserted her. And Skorky.

"I'll miss her," she whispered.

"I know." His arms tightened around her. "So will I."

She squeezed him tight and waited for the trip to complete. Being snug tight against his chest made it easier. "Sure wish we were going home."

His arms tightened.

Storey rested her cheek against his chest. How nice to be held by him again. He smelled so masculine and seemed so strong. It had been a long time for her. She could hardly remember what it was like to be in a relationship. As for her old boyfriend, well, she could hardly remember what he looked like either. Eric had taken his spot in her life.

"Are you okay?"

With a warm sigh, she rubbed her cheek against his chest. His arms squeezed and released. She did it again. He gripped her tight. "Witch, that tickles."

She giggled. "Sorry. Shouldn't tease you."

"Teasing is fine, but I'd just as soon be back in one of our dimensions where we might be able to do a little more than tease," he responded gently.

Storey cuddled closer. She hadn't known Eric long enough to be comfortable taking the next step in their relationship. But she wasn't far off. She'd almost made it there with her ex before he'd moved.

The black mist seemed to last forever. Considering this was a short hop distance-wise, not even leaving the dimension, she didn't understand why it hadn't been a short port. Sometimes though, it seemed like the Internet; the more users, the slower the speed.

Although there was only she and Eric traveling here at the moment, there could be any number of people traveling this way in Eric's dimension. And hadn't Paxton said something about still having trouble with tears and gates?

Finally the mist lowered. Storey found herself regretting it. The tiny space was peaceful, almost intimate in a way. As if there were no other beings, no other pressing issues to deal with – just the two of them.

"Looks like we're back to saving the world again." Storey did a slow turn to make sure they were alone. She kind of recognized the area, but couldn't be totally sure. A group of trees lined the left side of the meadow they now occupied, and she thought the creek would be down a ways but in the same direction. "Can we determine where your father is from here?"

"I think so. Being the Councilman he has a tracker chip embedded in his arm. It was done decades ago. With any luck, it's still active and the codex can read it. It's always an iffy thing in another dimension as you don't know what might have been screwed up with all the traveling. The energy is going to affect it somehow, at least over time. This is my father's first offworld travel though, so it should be okay."

"Let's check first." She kept an eye out as they walked toward the trees again. Seemed like that's always the first thing they did when they arrived at one of these dimensions. Still, shelter was shelter.

After what seemed like a long time, but was probably only minutes, he said, "Got it."

Storey tilted her head, hearing a steady beat coming from his arm. "Straight ahead."

At the trees, they stopped to check the beacon again. Following the same path, they came to the creek. Storey had a drink, but kept glancing around, ever mindful of the women who'd come upon them last time. Neither of them saw anyone walking around this time, and the tracking system was leading them back to the caves in the cliff.

"Well, at least we know we're in the right place." Storey ran a hand over her hair, wishing for a long hot soak and for this to all be over with. She was feeling melancholic over leaving Tammy behind.

As they approached the cliff's edge, they stopped at the same bunch of trees as last time. She surveyed the cliff dwellings, thankful the sun was behind clouds. "The place looks deserted."

"I wish, but so not likely," Eric snorted. "I sent a message to Paxton. Haven't heard back from him yet."

"We could use that backup team."

"I know. I asked. We need to have portals out at the ready this time, too."

Storey, winced, remembering how they'd had to jump, or in her case tumble, through the last portal as the Louers rushed them. "Yeah, I'd like to not have a repeat of last time, thank you."

"Me too. We'll wait here a bit longer until we hear from Paxton."

"In that case, there is something I need to ask the stylus. I should have asked him earlier." She plunked down on the ground, and removed the readymade portals she'd stashed in there and some blank paper. "Stylus, we need to fix the portal from this dimension to the Louers' old dimension. Then Tammy's father will remain the leader and these people can travel back and forth at will."

Yes.

Immediately Storey's hand flashed and danced on the paper. She watched, fascinated, as her stylus created something so advanced and difficult in mere seconds, that it was more like science fiction to her than reality. Moments later, her hand stilled.

"Is it done?"

Yes.

She gave Eric a wide smile. "We're good."

Eric crouched down to stare at the mess on her paper. "Does that mean anything to you?"

Giving the paper some serious study time, she finally shook her head. "Not at all." She turned the paper around slowly, looking for anything identifiable within the weird scribbles. Nothing. "Stylus, is the portal now functional?"

Yes.

"Can you tell Tammy's father that the portal works?"

A weird buzzing filled the air.

"It can't do that. Can it?" Eric's puzzled voice spoke

right at her ear.

"I have no idea. I was going to ask it to write a letter and explain everything about Tammy and the portal, but…" the buzzing became louder and louder. Just as she was ready to clap her hands over her ears, the noise stopped.

She exchanged a surprised look with Eric. Cautiously, she asked, "Stylus, what was that all about?"

I spoke with the leader.

"Um, just like that? You can communicate with him? Why did you not say so earlier?" she asked in exasperation. "We could have told them about Tammy before. And set up a way to return her."

Yes. I, too, am a Louer.

She exchanged an irritated look with Eric. She'd have to think on the implications of this. Later. "So does he understand about Tammy and the fixed broken portal? About our visit and the new dimension?" It sounded too good to be true, but given all the other things the stylus had done, it seemed on par.

Yes.

"And he won't interfere with our mission to rescue my father?" Eric asked, doubt, turning to almost disbelief in his voice.

No. He will deal with the other group after we leave. Now that the portal works, he will be able to get their tools and the rest of their people over.

Eric pursed his lips. "Really. And they will leave my dimension alone?"

He says they want nothing to do with your people. They want to be left alone to build a new life here.

"I'd like that, too," Storey muttered. "Now we just have to muzzle your father so he stops interfering with the

Louers!"

That was the leader's request. Take your father home and keep him there.

"And we'd be happy to. Just as soon as we can rescue the Councilman." She sighed. "Stylus, please make sure Tammy knows how much we miss her." Her stomach growled. Talk about a reminder of Tammy. Storey groaned silently. She'd love a home cooked meal right now. Her mom was a great cook; she just didn't have much time or inclination to do much these days. Come to think of it, her mom hadn't dated in years, either.

Storey had been grateful to not have to deal with a long line of "uncles" but still, she had to wonder if her mom was happy or if she'd abstained from the dating scene on purpose as Storey had gotten older. She'd never taken the time to ask her. *There's nothing like having your perception of reality blown apart by crossing dimensions to make you take a hard look at who you are.*

"Heavy thoughts?"

Storey glanced up. "Lots. Just looking back on my life."

He grimaced. "I've been doing a bit of that myself. Once you uncover one lie, like my perception of my father, it's almost impossible to not dissect the rest of your life looking for more."

"I think you should contact Paxton again."

Eric frowned. "I've been contacting him every ten minutes. There's no answer."

Storey frowned. Figures. "So are we going in without them? Waiting longer? What could be wrong?" She was pulling out her stylus as she spoke. Grabbing one of the small pieces of blank paper, she asked the stylus, "Contact Paxton and find out what the holdup is, please."

Her right hand jerked immediately. Even after all this time, she still watched in fascination as the stylus communicated through to Paxton in an alternate dimension.

He's under attack.

"What?" Eric stared at her before pulling the sketchbook away to read the message himself. "Surely not from the Louers again, right?"

At Eric's question, the stylus jumped to answer. *Yes, they attacked after you left. They are holding the Councilman hostage in the new dimension.*

"If we rescue the hostage, will that stop their attack on Eric's dimension?"

No. They are there now.

Eric, anger glinting deep in his eyes, added, "That also means that the force here is small. We will have an easier time rescuing him."

"Sure, but why would we?" she couldn't help but mutter.

"I understand your feelings, but imagine what trouble he could stir up for us if left here for a week or two."

She'd give him that point. "So what do you want to do? Go home and help fight the Louers off, stay here and rescue your father?"

"Damn."

Storey's gaze widened. A hint of laugher sounded in her voice as she said, "Now I know you're upset. That's like the third time I've ever heard you swear."

He frowned at her. "Now is hardly the time."

Storey sat back down. "Stylus, how many Louers are left guarding the Councilman?"

There are twelve adults here.

Twelve. That wasn't so bad. "What about women and

children?"

There are no children here and that count includes the fe-males. They are guards in this group.

"The stylus has to be communicating telepathically with the Louers to know this stuff." Eric stared at Storey and her sheet of paper.

"That would mean he's still more person than comput-er – right?" The concept confused her. She'd assumed and was sure that she'd clarified the issue at one point. She'd believed the stylus was more computer thingy than alive. That assumption made it easier for her to deal with the concept of the prisoners held indefinitely inside the pencil.

An intense humming filled the air. This time there was an unpleasantness to it. Storey looked around uneasily. Up to this point, the humming had always had a benign feeling to it. "Eric, the buzzing is stronger."

"Yeah. I'm hearing it, myself." His voice was grim, his eyes never still, darting from place to place. "Are they coming toward us, then?"

"I'm wondering. At only twelve left behind, I doubt they are all approaching." Turning the stylus around in her fingers, she asked, "Stylus, are the Louers approaching us?"

Yes. A group of four is approaching from inside the cliff.

Storey's voice rose as she bolted to her feet. "How did they find out about us?"

The stylus's answer came quickly.

I told them.

Eric's jaw clenched. Storey felt betrayal sweep through her, although she fought it, didn't want to believe it would have done such a thing.

It's the fastest way to find your father and get you home to help the rest of your world.

Storey took a deep breath and let it out slowly. She gazed into Eric's furious eyes. "We might not like it, but he's right." A muscle twitched on the corner of Eric's jaw. "If we can rescue him, we can jump through a portal together."

"We *had* the element of surprise. Not now. We have portals but only for the moment. Remember last time?"

"Shit." She didn't know what to do. "Stylus, how can we get in and out without being caught?"

Port in.

"What?"

Port to where you found Tammy.

Her mouth dropped. She should have considered that. With Eric supporting the paper on his back, she quickly drew an image of the cave where they'd rescued Tammy from. "Almost done."

"Then draw faster and make sure you're drawing this location or something similar so we can get out cleaner."

"Except for the time travel issue."

"Right. So scrap the second portal then. We'll codex out."

Her hand flew as her pulse screamed at them to run.

Eric continued to talk while she worked. "We need to search for the stuff they stole from us last time. Though I've been thinking. Would they have gone through a portal or used a codex when they didn't know where they were going or how to get back?"

She frowned. There's no way she would.

Eric twisted slightly to see her. "We used the one portal to go to my world, remember. The others, although which ones I don't remember exactly, would have taken them to your world."

"And they would have had to deal with the time travel

issue," Storey said, not raising her head. "Maybe they used your father's codex? With his help?"

Finally she finished. It felt like a half hour but she'd whipped the sketches together in minutes.

The buzzing in her ears was getting louder. Almost a bee sound. Incredibly hard to listen to. She smacked the side of her head. "They have to be close. Let's go."

As if the approaching Louers could sense what they were planning, the noise became deafening.

"Hurry, they're trying to knock us out before we can leave."

Storey dropped the portal on the ground, almost pushing Eric into it. He grabbed her hand. "I want you with me. Let's not get separated."

Warmth wrapped around her heart. "I'm here. I have to make sure we grab this portal as we go through. We can't take any more chances."

The pressure in her ears built up. She gasped at the pain, dropping to her knees at the edge of the paper. "Go, go. They're almost here."

Holding her left hand, the corner of the paper clenched in her right, Eric jumped in and pulled her with him.

Blackness surged through her consciousness as she fell into the hole.

CHAPTER 17

SOMEONE MOANED.

Storey wished they'd stop. Her headache boomed deep inside. "Easy, Storey." Eric's voice split right through her skull. She shuddered.

"It's over now, but we almost didn't make it. We're still feeling the effects of their telepathic weapon."

Storey sat up in a panic, grabbing her head as it threatened to explode. "Did the portal come with us?"

The large sheet of paper landed in the dirt in front of her. Groaning, she dropped back to the ground. "Thank heavens. I don't think I'd be able to run anywhere right now."

"Too bad," snapped an angry voice behind them. "You took so long to get here, we don't have a choice. We have to leave now."

Storey closed her eyes. Damn. The Councilman still lived.

"Hello, father." Eric struggled to his feet.

Storey didn't bother. Besides, she wasn't sure she could. The pounding inside her skull had eased slightly, but not enough to make movement a good idea yet.

"Storey? You can recuperate back home."

Home? Her eyelids popped open. "That much effort might be possible."

"Better yet," the Councilman snapped, "we leave you here. You're responsible for this mess. Let's go, Eric."

"No." Eric's harsh voice left no doubt about his seriousness. "She comes with us or I leave you here."

Storey's gaze landed on the Councilman's face long enough to see the hate glazing his eyes. He obviously hadn't come to terms with her presence in his world. At least back at Paxton's lab, she knew they'd take care of him. With false energy, she struggled to her feet, but was forced to stay bent over for a long moment to adjust to being vertical.

"Can you see any of the other codexes? Portals?" She studied around the dark space. It appeared empty. But in the darkness, who could tell for sure. And they didn't have time for a full search right now.

"Father, is there anything left here with you?"

"No, they didn't understand and ruined them with water and they are wearing the codexes. That's how they went home." He snorted as he scrambled to his feet. "They didn't need much guidance on their usage."

Storey exchanged an appalled look with Eric. How much did the Louers know of Toran technology after their session with Eric's father? "If Paxton can shut them down that might be the easiest way to deal with any that can't be retrieved."

"And if he can't?" Eric glared at his father. "Did you really help them use the codexes…against your own people?" His jaw worked furiously. "Have you so little regard for your home? That you would bring something like this on them?"

The Councilman turned his back on Storey to glower at Eric. He sniffed hard and lifted his nose into the air. "It was the only way to secure my safety."

"Jesus," Storey muttered under her breath. "Eric, are you prepared to trust his word about the portals and codexes?"

Running a hand through his short cropped hair, Eric frowned. He walked the small space where his father had been held. There were small pieces of paper on the ground at the doorway to the next cavern, soaked and damaged beyond use. "He's correct about these." Eric pointed to the fragments. "Let's hope Paxton *can* disable the remaining codexes."

Storey walked over, the portal in her hand. "I'll ask the stylus to disable any still functioning portals as well. Soon as we get somewhere safe."

"That makes sense."

"Enough already," snapped the Councilman. "The guards will be here any minute. Let's go."

Even as the words left his mouth they heard heavy sounds of someone running. Then another set of running footsteps.

"Shit." Storey stepped back to give Eric room. "Hurry."

Eric bent over in agony, his hands clasped to his ears.

"My head. The pain. I can't think."

That same horrible noise built up inside Storey's head. Damn the Louers' and their secret weapon. "We have to go. Punch the codes." Storey gasped as the pain increased.

"Hurry up," snapped the Councilman. The noise twisted his features, but didn't seem to be crippling him the same as Eric and her. "Why can't we travel by codex? Or portals?"

Time. That's why they couldn't go by portal. "It has to be codex. Time is a problem with portals." Storey yelled to be heard over the pounding in her head.

Eric's gaze widened as he understood her. "Right. I forgot." He took a deep breath, pulled back his sleeve and tapped a sequence of numbers.

The Councilman stepped closer, his nervous gaze searching the darkness around them. Hissing, he said, "Hurry."

"It takes a moment." Eric's face twisted against the unbearable noise. He bent over gasping for breath. Mist swirled up from the ground. Storey struggled to remain conscious as pain turned her world black. She didn't know how Eric was faring or why the Councilman seemed unaffected. Unless his sheer size had something to do with it.

Gratefully, she realized that the higher the black mist, the less the noise penetrated. It didn't take long before she could stand up straight. Over Eric's shoulder she watched several Louer guards race into the chamber. "Uh, Eric? How far does the mist have to climb before it's too late to reverse?"

She nodded behind him. He turned his head, his shoulders relaxed. "It's too late now."

The Councilman glared at her. "Don't be telling her any of our secrets."

"It's hardly a secret, Father. Besides, it's nothing to what you've told them."

Keeping a wary eye on the two Louers, Storey held her breath until the mist blocked her view. They were safe.

The black mist was damn freaky. She didn't understand how the system worked. If she was in the middle of the haze, would it only transport part of her? If the Louers had tried to jump in, would only part of them make it? That thought shook her.

Still, they'd gotten away clean. Eric was here with her, Tammy was home and they were even bringing the Councilman back. There might be some skirmishing going on in Eric's dimension, but his people were perfectly capable of taking care of that problem now. Maybe she could finally go home. In truth, she wanted a hug from her mother. She couldn't believe how much she'd missed her.

The mist closed over her head.

"Thank heavens for that," she whispered.

"We're fine. Almost home now."

She closed her eyes and waited for the endless darkness to lighten. And waited. "Eric?"

"Another moment. The codex has stopped signaling."

His comforting tone of voice reassured her almost as much as his words. She breathed a sigh of relief. "Good, I was afraid something else had gone wrong."

"No. Everything's fine. Almost there."

The stiffness eased from her shoulders and her insides relaxed.

Just then two hands reached out and gave her a shove – hard. She lost her balance.

A shocked shriek escaped her.

ERIC REACHED OUT to grab her and yelled, "Storey? What's the matter?"

There was only silence.

And empty space.

Stay tuned for the next in the series!
Darkest Designs, Book III
Or enjoy a different series!

Author's Note

Thank you for reading Deadly Designs! If you enjoyed my book, I'd appreciate it if you'd leave a review.

Dear reader,

I love to hear from readers, and you can contact me at my website: www.dalemayer.com or at my Facebook author page. To be informed of new releases and special offers, sign up for my newsletter or follow me on BookBub. And if you are interested in joining Dale Mayer's Reader Group, here is the Facebook sign up page.
http://geni.us/DaleMayerFBGroup

Cheers,
Dale Mayer

Gem Stone (A Gemma Stone Mystery)

A juvie kid trying to stay on the right path stumbles into trouble…

Gemma takes her camera everywhere. From juvie hall to a halfway home, the new hobby gives her a focus she'd never had before and… hope in a future. Until she takes pictures of something that could get her killed.

And not just her…after she and another juvie girl are chased by a stranger to the halfway home that same night, the other girl goes missing and Gemma knows she needs help. But who can she trust?

Not the authorities that's for sure. Trusting them is impossible for a girl with her damaged history, and besides, who cares about a troubled kid…especially when trouble just naturally seems to find her.

In Cassie's Corner

Faith and loyalty are tested as a young girl learns what it is to believe – in herself, in her friends, and in life after death.

Cassie's best friend, bad boy Todd, is gone. Gone as in dead. Gone as in he's now a ghost.

But she doesn't realize that when he wakes her in her bedroom and begs her not to believe what they say about him. It's not until the next day when her parents tell her about the accident that she learns the truth…

The police believe Todd was living up to the family name, drinking and driving and coming to a predictable end. It's up to her to find out the truth and clear his name.

Todd is shocked at his sudden change in circumstances…and angry. He struggles with his new ghostly reality, realizing all he's lost as he watches his brother build a relationship with Cassie as the two pair up to find out what really happened to him.

The truth isn't always pretty, and Cassie has to be stronger than ever before. Especially when the whole world seems to be against her.

About the Author

Dale Mayer is a *USA Today* best-selling author, best known for her SEALs military romances, her Psychic Visions series, and her Lovely Lethal Garden cozy series. Her contemporary romances are raw and full of passion and emotion (Broken But … Mending, Hathaway House series). Her thrillers will keep you guessing (Kate Morgan, By Death series), and her romantic comedies will keep you giggling (*It's a Dog's Life*, a stand-alone novella; and the Broken Protocols series, starring Charming Marvin, the cat).

Dale honors the stories that come to her—and some of them are crazy, break all the rules and cross multiple genres!

To go with her fiction, she also writes nonfiction in many different fields, with books available on résumé writing, companion gardening, and the US mortgage system. All her books are available in print and ebook format.

Connect with Dale Mayer Online

Dale's Website – www.dalemayer.com
Twitter – @DaleMayer
Facebook Page – geni.us/DaleMayerFBFanPage
Facebook Group – geni.us/DaleMayerFBGroup
BookBub – geni.us/DaleMayerBookbub
Instagram – geni.us/DaleMayerInstagram
Goodreads – geni.us/DaleMayerGoodreads
Newsletter – geni.us/DaleNews

Also by Dale Mayer

Published Adult Books:

Psychic Vision Series

Tuesday's Child

Hide'n Go Seek

Maddy's Floor

Garden of Sorrow

Knock, Knock…

Rare Find

Eyes to the Soul

Now You See Her

Shattered

Into the Abyss

Psychic Visions Books 1–3

Psychic Visions Books 4–6

Psychic Visions Books 7–9

By Death Series

Touched by Death – Part 1

Touched by Death – Part 2

Touched by Death – Parts 1&2

Haunted by Death

Chilled by Death

By Death Books 1–3

Second Chances…at Love Series

Second Chances – Part 1

Second Chances – Part 2

Second Chances – complete book (Parts 1 & 2)

Charmin Marvin Romantic Comedy Series

Broken Protocols

Broken Protocols 2

Broken Protocols 3

Broken Protocols 3.5

Broken Protocols 1-3

Broken and… Mending

Skin

Scars

Scales (of Justice)

Broken but… Mending 1-3

Glory

Genesis

Tori

Celeste

Glory Trilogy

Biker Blues

Biker Blues: Morgan, Part 1

Biker Blues: Morgan, Part 2

Biker Blues: Morgan, Part 3

Biker Baby Blues: Morgan, Part 4

Biker Blues: Morgan, Full Set

Biker Blues: Salvation, Part 1

Biker Blues: Salvation, Part 2

Biker Blues: Salvation, Part 3

Biker Blues: Salvation, Full Set

SEALs of Honor

Mason: SEALs of Honor, Book 1

Hawk: SEALs of Honor, Book 2

Dane: SEALs of Honor, Book 3

Swede: SEALs of Honor, Book 4

Shadow: SEALs of Honor, Book 5

Cooper: SEALs of Honor, Book 6

Markus: SEALs of Honor, Book 7

Evan: SEALs of Honor, Book 8

Mason's Wish: SEALs of Honor, Book 9

SEALs of Honor, Books 1–3

SEALs of Honor, Books 4–6

Collections

Dare to Be You...

Dare to Love...

Dare to be Strong...

RomanceX3

Standalone Novellas

It's a Dog's Life

Riana's Revenge

Published Young Adult Books:

Family Blood Ties Series

Vampire in Denial

Vampire in Distress

Vampire in Design

Vampire in Deceit

Vampire in Defiance

Vampire in Conflict

Vampire in Chaos

Vampire in Crisis

Vampire in Control

Vampire in Charge

Family Blood Ties Set 1–3

Family Blood Ties Set 1–5

Family Blood Ties Set 4–6

Family Blood Ties Set 7–9

Sian's Solution – A Family Blood Ties Short Story

Design series

Dangerous Designs

Deadly Designs

Darkest Designs

Design Series Trilogy

Standalone

In Cassie's Corner

Gem Stone (a Gemma Stone Mystery)

Time Thieves

Published Non-Fiction Books:

Career Essentials

Career Essentials: The Résumé

Career Essentials: The Cover Letter

Career Essentials: The Interview

Career Essentials: 3 in 1

9 781988 315980